ANNIE MOORE
NEW YORK CITY GIRL

For my daughter Roisin

ANNIE MOORE
NEW YORK CITY GIRL

The fifteen-year-old who was the very first immigrant to land at Ellis Island, New York, has now become a young woman of twenty, and has returned to New York after a stay in the wild west. She is excited at the prospect of spending more time with Mike Tierney, the young man she loves, and while Mike is campaigning in a presidential election, Annie fights for women's right to vote. Then, just when life seems to be going right, war intervenes, taking Mike far away, into great danger. Annie discovers that there is so.. as well as joy in growing up...

Annie Moore
New York City
Girl

by

Eithne Loughrey

Dales Large Print Books
Long Preston, North Yorkshire,
BD23 4ND, England.

British Library Cataloguing in Publication Data.

Loughrey, Eithne
    Annie Moore New York City girl.

    A catalogue record of this book is
    available from the British Library

    ISBN   1-84262-448-2 pbk
    ISBN   978-1-84262-448-7 pbk

Published in Large Print 2006 by arrangement with
Mercier Press

Dales Large Print is an imprint of Library Magna Books Ltd.

Printed and bound in Great Britain by
T.J. (International) Ltd., Cornwall, PL28 8RW

3157233 2

CONTENTS

1 Home at Last   9

2 Working in the City Store   24

3 A Protest on Polling Day   48

4 Sophia and the Bright Angels   65

5 Changes and Partings   84

6 Mike Breaks the News   108

7 Tragedy at the Refuge   127

8 News from the Front   148

9 The War Is Over   171

10 The Biggest Adventure of All   190

Epilogue   203

1

HOME AT LAST

Clickety-clack, clickety-clack, clickety-clack ... the train bearing Annie eastwards lulled her into a dreamlike trance as she gazed out over the parched prairie landscape, which was dotted here and there with sunflowers, raising their wilting heads to wish her Godspeed. It was July and coming close to harvest-time. It had been a good year and there would be bumper crops, Carl had said.

Carl. Annie shifted uncomfortably in her seat as she thought back on her last weeks in Nebraska. She was learning that, much as you might wish to do so, you couldn't tidy people away in cubbyholes the way you could books or clothes. And Carl had no wish to be tidied away, she had found. He

9

had said he would come to New York the following year to see her and that he still hoped she might love him. When parting from her in Lincoln a few days previously, he had presented her with a tiny gold locket with his picture in it.

Carl was handsome and fun to be with and she would be forever grateful to him for saving her life as he had last summer, but he didn't make her heart beat faster the way Mike Tierney did. Ever since Mike had come to visit in Lincoln – and that was nearly a year ago now – Annie was certain that she loved Mike and that no one else could mean to her what he did.

She could tell that Aunt Marthe understood how she felt, even though they had hardly exchanged two words about it. Even though Carl was her nephew and she would have liked it if Annie had chosen to remain in Nebraska.

'You're sure doin' the right thing, young lady, headin' back east. Your family must have missed you somethin' terrible. It's about time you got back to them.' Aunt Marthe had said to her.

What Annie didn't know was that Aunt Marthe had watched her with Mike when he had visited Lincoln last year, and it had been abundantly clear to her that the young couple were deeply in love.

It was such a relief now to sit in the train returning east with all goodbyes said. It had been especially sad to bid farewell to Ellen, Dan and the babies some weeks back. 'If it wasn't for that Mike Tierney, I'd never let go of you, lass,' Ellie had smiled at Annie through her tears as they clung together on the railway platform at Kimball. And although Annie promised to come back to see them before long, they both knew in their hearts that she would not be taking such a very long trip again for some time.

Then there were the goodbyes at Miller's Creek, where she had known nothing but kindness. Gertrude and Eric had even hosted a little farewell party for her. And as for Aunt Marthe herself, who had looked after Annie like a mother during the past year in Lincoln, it had been a real wrench to part from her.

What wonderful friends she had made in her two-year stay in Nebraska, she reflected. Life would be very different back in New York. So many thousands of people, yet so few likely to become friends. Out here in the West, people had no choice but to befriend each other. Life was so difficult, there was no question of being choosy. She recalled the months she'd spent out on the prairie with Ellie and Dan in the sod-house with not a soul in sight for weeks on end, so that when neighbours did happen by, they were treated like royalty.

Annie smiled to herself as she recalled the time she and Ellie had been cut off by a blizzard from getting help with little Scott's birth and Annie had just had to get on with it. Of all her adventures in the West, that was without doubt the most exciting and the most frightening. Oh, except for the time she was caught in the prairie fire with Carl and he'd saved both their lives by lighting a backfire.

It was time to look to the future now: a future that she dearly hoped would be shared with Mike. This made her smile and then sigh as she reflected that Mike would not be among those to welcome her to New York when she arrived. He would already have left for Chicago, where the Democratic convention was about to take place. It was at the time of the last presidential election that she had really come to know him, she recalled. She had been a raw recruit, one of the many young people Mike had organised to distribute political leaflets in the weeks leading up to the election.

It was on that occasion also that she had first met Molly. They had taken to each other instantly and had become firm friends. And soon, to her great joy, they would become sisters. Molly had become betrothed to Annie's brother Tom last Christmas and they planned to wed in a year or so. In the meantime, the plan was that Molly would give up her teaching job in Brooklyn, where her family lived, and move to New York to be nearer to Tom. Here she hoped to take up another job and she and Annie planned to go into lodgings together. Perhaps they would take a flat, something that many modern young working women did nowadays.

Mike had written to her of his excitement at being chosen as one of the team to travel to Chicago for the convention. It was almost certain that the famous Nebraskan senator William Jennings Bryan would be nominated as the Democratic candidate in Chicago. How thrilled all her friends in Nebraska would be to have their very own candidate running for president of the United States. And how lucky she was to have actually met the great man last autumn when he had spoken at a political rally in Lincoln. How impressed Father had been when she had written to him about that.

How I wish I could be at Grand Central Station with the family to meet you, Annie, Mike had written in his last letter, *but I have no choice but to go to Chicago. I will be back within the week. I long to see you,* he added.

After an initial stab of disappointment, Annie was a little relieved that he would not be there when she arrived. She did not want her reunion with Mike to take place in the company of her family. She would prefer to see him alone. Excited at the prospect of seeing him again, she felt unaccountably shy now that the time had come. Although his letters had been long and regular, they were always full of his political doings and of his work as a tailor but short on sentiment.

That wasn't strictly true, she thought, recalling that on her nineteenth birthday last January, he had sent her a love note written in verse, which had revived her flagging hopes. But that was six months ago and of late she had begun to wonder whether his visit to Lincoln had ever really taken place.

Besides, she wanted to have an opportunity to explain to her parents that she and Mike would now be walking out together. This was one bit of news she knew her father would surely not object to. He thought highly of Mike and followed his political doings with a lively interest. Annie knew that he might not find it so easy if it was Carl she was bringing home. She smiled as she imagined his reaction to someone like Carl: 'A cowboy, Annie, I'm telling ya, he's nothing but a cowboy.' Her father had never lost his Cork accent in all his years in America, and Annie guessed he never would.

Suddenly she had an overwhelming urge to see her family again. It had been so long, and when she had left New York two years ago she had not been at all sure that she ever wanted to return. The months before her departure had been so fraught, what with losing her job at the Van der Leutens' and then her certainty at the time that Mike loved somebody else.

Looking back on it all now, she realised how far she'd come since those days. She had grown up so much. She had studied hard in the past year, completing her course at Lincoln University, which qualified her to work as an assistant teacher. She was now truly independent and had every prospect of getting a job in New York, where – according to Mike – they were crying out for teachers. Besides, she had learned so much about life out in Nebraska. It had been good to get away from her family and test her mettle. Returning to New York now, she felt able for whatever life threw at her.

Annie slept soundly that night, lulled by the rhythmic rocking of the sturdy express bearing her homewards.

It was two full days before the train finally drew up on the platform at Grand Central Station in New York.

'Annie, Annie ... at last...' Mother, weighed down by baby Elizabeth – the latest arrival to the Moore family – pushed forwards through the crowds and flung her free arm around her eldest daughter. Annie eyed her new baby sister with delight and looked around to see her entire family gathered to meet her. How the boys had grown! She just could not believe it. Anthony was now towering over her, and Philip was nearly as tall as she was. Tom had changed least, still looking the dapper young man about town, but he'd filled out a little and looked more prosperous. And little Pat, no longer the baby, stood sturdily holding his father's hand, gazing solemnly at this sister who'd become a stranger. And dear Uncle Charlie and Auntie Norah, the same as ever, their faces beaming with happiness at the sight of her.

What an excited group they made as they clustered about her, their beloved Annie, returned home at long last.

Any misgivings she'd had about returning to New York disappeared instantly at the sight of them all. The round of welcome hugs over, the happy group left the station and set off for home.

The first few days of her return were ones of sheer enjoyment for Annie. She had a lot of catching up to do. Despite the fact that her parents had moved into a new, larger apartment near Delancey Street, space was still at a premium since the arrival of baby Elizabeth, and Annie had moved in straight away with Auntie Norah and Uncle Charlie in Cherry Street. However, this was only to be a temporary arrangement until she and Molly set up house together: an adventure she was greatly looking forward to.

Molly had landed a new job in a midtown kindergarten and would start work there at the end of the summer vacation. In the meantime, to enable her to live in town and pay rent, she had taken a job as a clerk in a bookstore. Annie, she said, would need to start looking for work straight away. She had written her friend a welcome-home note, promising to visit in a few days, when they could go flat-hunting together.

Annie enjoyed a long heart-to-heart talk with her parents and found them still planning to move out of New York in the next couple of years.

'Once we have Philip settled, we'll go,' they told her. 'We want to bring the little ones up far away from the city.'

Father had been reading about the territory of Arizona, down near Mexico.

'There are going to be great opportunities out there,' he told his daughter. 'We might be able to start some class of a business. Charlie and Norah are thinking of coming with us,' he added.

Annie was astounded. She had never thought of her parents as adventurous in any way and yet here they were, planning on going halfway across America in search of a new life. She had assumed they would stay in New York for the rest of their lives, or perhaps eventually go back to Ireland. But Arizona, she'd heard, was nothing but a desert, full of cactus plants, rattlesnakes and scorpions.

Her father snorted when she voiced this opinion. 'Naw, girl, where do you get your ideas from? It's a grand climate. Be good for your bronchitis, so it would – better than this place. Besides, it's got the railroad now as far as Phoenix, and they even have a university at Tucson. No, Arizona will be the place to be, you mark my words. They say it will become a state one of these days.'

'But tell us your news, *a stór.* What are you planning to do with yourself now that you're back?' Mother, ever anxious to avoid a clash between fiery-natured Father and head-strong Annie, changed the subject swiftly. Besides, she hadn't quite come around to abandoning the life to which she'd become accustomed in exchange for the western adventure envisaged by Father. He would have to work hard to win her over.

'You know, of course, I'll be looking for work right away,' Annie began, knowing that this was her chance to tell them about Mike, yet hesitating.

'Faith, then, and I believe there's a certain young man who has been giving you advice on that score,' her father remarked with a sudden twinkle in his eye.

Annie blushed. Judging by their smiles, her parents must have known all along that she and Mike had been corresponding all these months. They had known of his visit to Nebraska accompanying William Jennings

Bryan the previous autumn because she had written to them about it, but she had not confided that during that visit their relationship had undergone a change, from that of family friend to sweetheart.

'Well...' she started, confused. 'Yes, as a matter of fact, Mike and I have been writing to each other. And yes, he thinks I will certainly find a teaching job here.'

Gathering from the look they exchanged that they had guessed at the nature of her feelings for Mike, she added, 'I think me and Mike will be seeing a little more of each other than we used to.'

'We thought that might be the case.' Father nodded amicably, much to Annie's relief. 'Faith, and maybe you won't be seeing as much of him as you think with the presidential primaries coming up in November. It's likely that that Bryan fella from Nebraska will be nominated in Chicago this week and if he is, Mike will be workin' fit to bust a gut for the next while.'

Father's words were prophetic, but right

now Annie didn't care. She knew Mike would be based in New York because his job was there, and they would manage to see each other somehow. She just longed to see him again, and as her first week in New York drew to a close without a sight of him, she grew impatient.

Finally, arriving back at Cherry Street one afternoon after a busy day's flat-hunting with Molly, she spotted a familiar figure waiting by the stoop, hat in one hand and a huge bunch of flowers in the other.

She didn't hesitate for a moment. All shyness gone, she ran towards him. Simultaneously, Mike spotted Annie and stood with his arms outstretched. Clasping her close, he swung her around and around, both of them laughing with joy, until they all but collapsed on the sidewalk.

'At last,' breathed Mike into her hair, 'my girl is home.'

And from that moment, Annie knew that she truly was home.

That evening, the young couple made up

for the long months of separation. They had so much to tell each other, so much to catch up on that it was midnight before Annie got back to Cherry Street. As she skipped up the steps of the darkened building to her aunt and uncle's top-floor apartment, she reflected on how different life seemed now than it had two years previously. Then she had felt somehow disillusioned, and had been kept going only by thoughts of escape from this city. Now she felt life had everything to offer her. And it had.

2

WORKING IN THE CITY STORE

Number 47 St Mark's Place was all Annie and Molly could have dreamed it would be. On the top floor of a four-storey walk-up, their modest little apartment offered a fine view over the trees in Tompkin's Square Park. While they had the pain of having to climb four flights of stairs to reach it, they and the other top-floor tenants had the joy of being able to walk out onto the roof, where there was space to hang their washing out to dry and even sit and admire the view over the city on fine evenings. This was a godsend during the final weeks of that hot summer.

It reminded Annie of her early days in New York, when everyone in Monroe Street used to climb out onto the fire escapes to try to get a breath of air during the sizzling hot summer nights. Some even brought their bedding out and spent the night there.

They had been so lucky to find this flat, in the end managing to get it through a friend of Molly's father. In fact, if it had not been for his involvement, Annie's parents would have disapproved of such a scheme, much preferring to see their daughter stay on at Norah and Charlie's, or at least to be safely ensconced as a lodger in a respectable boarding house. However, they had finally been won over when they discovered that the other tenants were all young working women.

The landlady – who lived on the first floor – was pleasant enough and didn't interfere with them, as long as they paid their rent in time and obeyed the rules of the house. No late callers would be countenanced and gentlemen callers were forbidden at all times. Even Annie's father, coming to inspect the new premises his daughter was to occupy, had first to pass muster with Mrs Morrissey.

The idea that anyone would see Annie's father as a 'gentleman caller' made the girls giggle a good deal. But it also made them realise that any hopes they might have had of entertaining Mike and Tom were out of the question – unless, of course, they had a serious chaperone.

Both families contributed odds and ends of furniture and household goods for the flat and in no time they were comfortably established in what was, for both of them, their first independent grown-up home.

It's such fun to have our own place, Annie

wrote to Ellen after she had settled in:

We have two small bedrooms (really one divided in two) and a fair-sized living room with a stove. There's a bathroom on the same floor, which is a blessing and, best of all, a door opening on to the roof which on these stifling hot nights is a mercy. How I would love to show it to you. I think of you all busy as bees getting in the harvest and how I was helping you with it just a year ago. Much help I was! Part of me would love to be back there with you now, but that would mean I would have to be parted from Mike. He means so much to me, Ellie, and although he works so very hard that we do not get to see one another as much as we would wish, when we do meet we are so happy and don't waste a minute but tell each other everything and plan how we can be together.

I think I have hope of a position at last but it seems the job will not become vacant until January next so if they accept me I will have to find some other work until then.

It's good to be back in New York and exciting too because everyone's talking about who the new president will be, and of course I'm longing for it to be Mr Jennings Bryan, not just because I know you all wish for him to win – him being from Nebraska and all. Mike tells me great things about what he will do for the country. And he's younger than Mr McKinley and better-looking. They call him 'the boy wonder', although he sure doesn't look like a boy to me.

Molly and I are wishing we had the vote but there's no sign of that coming to pass. I have seen in Nebraska the way women can work and do everything that men do and it seems so unfair that they don't get any chance to share in running the country. I feel much madder about it now than I did a few years back and I intend to join Molly in the Women's Suffrage Association, who are trying very hard to get women the vote. First, however, I must find some work because the rent will have to be paid in three weeks' time and I have very little savings left.

Luck was on Annie's side again, as within days of writing to Ellie, Auntie Norah called around one evening and asked if she'd found a teaching job yet. When Annie explained the position, Norah smiled, saying, 'Well, I might have just the job to tide you over, for a while anyway.' Norah worked in the Millinery Department at A. & T. Stewart's Department Store.

'They need extra staff during the summer sales and it doesn't pay too bad. I am sure you would be equal to it.'

'Oh, Auntie, that would be marvellous.' Annie was excited at the prospect of working in one of New York's finest stores. Besides, it was only a short walk from where she now lived.

It was arranged that she would come in to see Miss Gilroy in the Personnel Department the following morning.

'Wear your best costume, Annie,' Norah advised. 'They like employees to look as smart as possible.'

Next morning, Annie presented herself bright and early at the vast department store on Broadway, between Ninth and Tenth Street. She had only been in A. & T. Stewart's once before, and as on her first visit, it took her breath away. The electric lighting illuminated everything so that the polished brass on the counters and on the staircases positively glittered. The aisles on the ground floor seemed to stretch for miles in every direction, with a variety of goods for sale that exceeded even the most ardent shopper's imagination. Her heart raced with excitement at the thought of working in such a place. The Personnel Department was on the sixth floor and she rode up in one of the splendid elevators, with its mirrors and polished wood interior and little velvet-covered stools. Asking to see Miss Gilroy, she was mighty grateful that Auntie Norah had warned her to appear at her best. All the women she had so far glimpsed in the store seemed so well-dressed that Annie felt dowdy, even in her best outfit.

She need not have worried too much. Miss Sadie Gilmore had a wise head on her, and when she saw the attractive and alert-looking young woman waiting to see her, she knew immediately that she would hire her. Some of the girls she'd interviewed the day before looked like right scatterbrains. But not this one. She had something special about her. She'd certainly put her on the shortlist.

'Now, I'm afraid that if we did take you, it would only be for a short spell,' she explained. 'Neither would you be assigned to any particular department. You would work as a floater, moving around to whatever department was busiest.'

'I would like that – it means I would get plenty of experience,' Annie replied, adding that she would be free to start immediately.

Promising to let her know the following day, Miss Gilroy shook Annie's hand and bid her goodbye.

Hoping earnestly that she had got the job, Annie wandered through the store, admiring the sophisticated appearance of the sales staff in every department – she thought they looked every bit as stylish as their wealthy clients. What fun she would have if she worked here. Even though it was still early morning, the place was abuzz with activity.

She called in to see Auntie Norah in the Millinery Department, enjoying the sight of her aunt at work in such an unfamiliar environment. Signalling to her niece to sit down on one of the settees, Norah continued to assist a rather portly lady in choosing a hat suitable for a society wedding.

This task took some time and Annie watched with interest as the woman tried on every hat in the house. Norah scurried from drawer to drawer to find the most suitable one. She was amazed at how long it took to find something to suit this customer and marvelled at her aunt's patience as hat after hat was tried on and turned down.

'This is a very important wedding,' the woman kept repeating petulantly. 'I simply *must* have the very best.'

Finally, having settled on an enormous peacock-blue tulle-swathed creation, the woman swept out, leaving details for its delivery to her home on Park Avenue later that day.

'Are they all as bad as that?' Annie asked

as Norah came swiftly to her side.

'Many are worse,' replied Auntie Norah, laughing. 'Tell me, did you get the position?'

'She is to let me know tomorrow. She said if they took me it would only be for a short time and I'd be a floater. Do you think I'll get it?'

Auntie Norah thought it likely that Annie would be taken on. Miss Gilroy would not have gone to the trouble of explaining the nature of the work if she hadn't wanted to hire her.

'Let's wait and see,' was all she said, however.

Auntie Norah's guess was astute and Annie was thrilled to get a letter by the next morning's post asking her to report for duty on the following Monday morning. The pay was low enough – four dollars a week – but it would do until she got a teaching job. She was to wear a smart black skirt and a white shirtwaist, the letter instructed, and her hair should be tied up neatly.

'I have a skirt that would be just right for

you, Annie,' Auntie Norah offered. 'It's too tight for me, I'm afraid, and it would save you buying a new one. And you have a couple of nice shirtwaists already, don't you?'

So come Monday morning, Annie joined the throngs of young working women making their way into shops, offices and factories all over the city.

She had been bidden to present herself to the fashion floor manager Miss Barton on her arrival. The very smart uniformed doorman who held open the great brass-handled doors for her to enter the store was able to direct her to Miss Barton's office on the fourth floor. Not waiting for the elevator, Annie hurried up the broad staircase wondering where she would be posted. Miss Barton, a very tall, elegant older woman peered at Annie short-sightedly through a pince-nez perched on the end of her nose.

'And who have we here?' she asked, gazing at Annie as if she were examining a very tiny insect from a long distance.

Just as well I brought the letter from Miss

Gilroy, thought Annie, trying not to feel intimidated. Miss Barton glanced at it and then smiled pleasantly, much to Annie's relief.

'Ah yes, I was expecting you. Now come with me and I will take you to the Dress Goods department,' she said, sweeping out of her office and setting off down the stairs to the first floor where already, despite the fact that the store had not yet opened to the public, staff were at their posts and ready for the day. Seeing Miss Barton approach all conversation ceased and an air of intense activity took over as bales of material were taken down from the high shelves ready for measuring on the counters.

The long glass-topped counters were manned by nearly all young women, mostly in their twenties, Annie guessed. The walls behind the counters were lined with shelves and drawers full of hosiery, collars, gloves and handkerchiefs. There were also rails and rails of mantles, costumes, gowns, skirts and shirt-waists of every size, colour and description.

Annie was introduced right away to a Miss Sarah Waters – a very pretty young woman and a friendly one too. She showed Annie around the department, explaining everything about the merchandise and showing her where everything was kept.

'You'll soon get used to it,' she said reassuringly. 'Perhaps today you might just rearrange these hosiery drawers and make sure all the sizes are in order. If there are any sizes missing just tell me and I will make sure to order some more. It's best if you do not serve customers until you become accustomed to everything,' she added. 'Most of the customers are nice and polite to deal with but some of them are right terrors.'

Thus, Annie spent her first day on these minor duties which gave her an opportunity to see what the work was like and indeed, to make the acquaintance of her colleagues. As the morning wore on, the store filled up and the girls fairly danced attendance on the ever-increasing number of customers attracted by the summer sales. The ting of the money tills became more and more frequent and Annie progressed to placing mark-down labels on incoming stock. She was glad to stop for a break at lunchtime and accompanied some of the other girls to the staff lunch room where she was introduced to young men and women from other departments.

The rest of the day passed pleasantly and by close of business she felt as if she had worked there for ever. She had enjoyed being surrounded by such an array of beautiful clothes and looked forward to the challenge of being allowed to deal with the customers and advise them on the kind of garments which would suit them.

'Now I can catch up on the fashions again,' she told Aunt Norah enthusiastically as they walked homewards together after work. 'It was so different in Nebraska with no time to think of dressing up finely. How Ellie would love a day there. I would have her looking a picture in no time.'

The days flew by and soon Annie was

serving customers and swapping stories about them with the other girls at lunchtime.

'It's much harder work than I had realised, but more interesting too.' Annie was describing her first week working in the Dress Goods Department at A. & T. Stewart's to the assembled family on Sunday afternoon. She and Mike had just arrived and Tom and Molly were also expected.

'Well, now you get to see what the rich can buy, but you won't have to work as hard as at the laundry, I'll be bound,' remarked Father, puffing on his pipe.

Mike remained silent and Annie determined to talk to him about it later, as, since she had taken the position, she had the feeling that somehow Mike slightly disapproved. She wondered why. Surely he didn't wish to see her back working in a laundry? However, Mother was avid for details of what the customers bought and how much they paid for this, that and the other item. She thought it all sounded wonderful, and said so.

'How I wish I had been able to work there when we first came to America,' she sighed, looking down at the sleeping baby in her arms. But she didn't really look too put out, Annie reflected. She lifted little Elizabeth gently from her mother's arms.

'By the time she grows up, she'll be able to do anything she wants,' she said softly. 'Perhaps even vote,' she added, smiling at Mike.

Soon afterwards, Tom and Molly arrived and the talk turned to politics. William Jennings Bryan had been nominated to run for the Democrats and Mike described how the Nebraska senator had fired his audience with excitement in Chicago.

'Imagine, if he becomes president, I'll be able to say I've met him!' Annie exclaimed.

'Well, you'll get another opportunity to see him,' said Mike. 'He's coming to New York in a few weeks' time and will speak at Madison Square Gardens. He's expected to be a great success.'

There followed some discussion of the coming rally in New York. Both Mike and

Tom would be working hard behind the scenes to organise it.

Later that evening, as Mike escorted Annie home through the heat-baked streets, she said, 'Mike, you don't seem altogether happy with me working at A. & T. Stewart's.'

Mike stopped and faced her, looking troubled. 'I'm not unhappy with it, Annie, and you must do what you wish, but I am disappointed you are not taking up the teaching after all your hard work. I think you'd be very good at it.'

'Oh, but I will, Mike. I hope to take up that position in St Margaret's when the vacancy comes up after Christmas.' She looked at him closely. 'There's something else, isn't there?'

'It's just that ... well, I thought you had had enough of the kind of people that patronise such a place. I didn't think you'd want to be exploited by them again.'

Annie felt her temper rising suddenly. 'No one is exploiting me, Mike. I am being paid quite well. And it's fun. Is it that it's not posh enough for you? Are you ashamed of me taking a position in a store?'

'That's silly of you, Annie. Of course not. I just feel you've developed beyond that. You could do so much more. And the workers there don't even belong to a union. I thought you cared about things like that.'

'Yes, I do, but it's surely not that important, is it? I am earning my living. That's what matters. I have to pay my rent and keep myself.' She turned away with an impatient gesture.

'I know that, Annie.' Mike turned her around and looked into her eyes. 'How can you say that I am ashamed of you? I am so proud of you. I just feel you are worth so much more. You are...' Mike paused, at a loss for words.

Dejected, they parted at the door of Annie's house. This was the first disagreement they'd had and it was all over nothing.

Annie thought about what Mike had said, but could not really make much sense of it. It was some months before the true import of his words hit home.

Annie was right. Working in A & T. Stewart's *was* fun, and over the next few weeks, as she was moved from one department to another, she became less intimidated by the palatial surroundings which had so overawed her at the beginning. She became more self-confident and at ease with her new workplace. When she entered the store each morning, she felt somehow as if she was leaving her real life behind and inhabiting a gilded fairyland. Gloriously illuminated, and ingeniously kept cool, in contrast with the inferno of the New York streets that summer, A. & T. Stewart's was a haven of comfort for both its employees and its customers.

Although the work was hard, she enjoyed the challenge and had plenty of time to make new acquaintances. Staff dined daily at the expense of their employers in the staff lunch room on the first floor. Leaving the store during the working day was frowned upon and required special permission. There was a sense of camaraderie among the many young people of around her own age on the staff and she enjoyed hearing them gossip about some of their more famous clients.

Betsy Blake had everyone in a flurry of excitement when she announced that Mrs Vanderbilt was expected to visit the Household Goods Department next morning.

'I know about it because I heard Mr Dunston tell Miss Barton to have someone special ready to assist her with her purchases,' reported Betsy. Pausing for effect, she added, 'And Miss Barton chose me. "Betsy," she said, "I know I can depend on you to put your best foot forward for Mr Stewart." "Of course, Miss," said I, "although I don't expect as how Mr Stewart would look twice at my best foot."'

General laughter greeted this performance – Betsy was a scream – and although she made a joke of it all, everyone knew that she was thrilled to be chosen. They all looked forward to hearing about Mrs Vanderbilt's purchases the following day.

Annie was equally thrilled as, not only did Mrs Vanderbilt spend quite some time in the Dress Goods Department after she had visited the Household Goods but she bid Annie look after her fur cloak while, assisted by Betsy, she was brought to the dressing-rooms to be fitted for a new gown.

There was a great air of excitement as this important customer had not been expected in their Department and one or two favoured assistants scurried to and fro with some of the most elegant gowns in stock. She eventually chose a white moiré silk tea-gown as well as a tailor-made paddock suit made of fine habit cloth, lined in silk with an extra full skirt. She was a fine-looking woman from what Annie could see for all that she was as imperious as a queen in her dealings with them. Although there was a general sigh of relief when she departed to her waiting carriage an hour later, the girls talked of nothing else for the rest of the day. Recalling the luxurious scent which permeated that lady's fur cloak, Annie daydreamed about what it would be like to live such a privileged life. It all seemed a long, long way from Nebraska's plains and prairies.

As the end of August approached and the summer rush abated, Annie waited for the day when she would be told she was no longer needed and given her notice. Then, one afternoon, she was summoned to Miss Gilroy's office.

'Come in and sit down, Miss Moore.' Miss Gilroy looked at Annie over her steel-rimmed spectacles and smiled.

'I hear good reports of your work,' she began, 'and I believe you would do well here at A. & T. Stewart's. Not everyone is suited to it, you know. However, I think you would fit in well. How would you like to stay on, in a permanent capacity?'

Annie was amazed. She had fully expected to be told that her employment at the store had come to an end.

'Well,' she stammered, 'I hadn't expected anything...' She blustered a bit, confused about how she felt and yet flattered to be asked.

However, such was Miss Gilroy's sense of confidence about the privilege she was conferring that she assumed Annie's hesitant reply was a delighted acceptance. Without waiting for further confirmation, she continued. 'Yes, I know I told you we could only keep you until the summer sales were over, and in general that is the case with staff taken on for that purpose, but we have a small number of vacancies coming up on our permanent staff and, as I said, you would be suitable for one of them. Tomorrow you will report to Ladies' Fashions.'

Without further ado, the interview was over and Annie found herself on her way downstairs in the elevator. She had mixed feelings. She was enjoying the work and there were still a few months to go before the teaching position at St Margaret's would become vacant. This would save her from having to take yet another position in the meantime, which was very convenient. Then why had she any misgivings? Many girls would jump at the opportunity of getting a permanent position at A. & T. Stewart's. It was a good job and now she would be paid a little better, too. But something was niggling at her.

Since her disagreement about it with Mike, they had not discussed it again and she had thought very little about it. Somehow, however, his words rankled and now came afresh to her mind. She knew he had nothing against A. & T. Stewart's especially. He would have felt the same had it been Bloomingdale's or Macy's. It was more his expectations of her that were involved. That in some way she was disappointing him.

However, Auntie Norah's delighted reaction when she called into Millinery on her way back was reassuring and Annie decided she had been worried about nothing. Mike would be pleased, surely, that she was so well thought of at A. & T. Stewart's. Permanent or not, she could always leave as soon as that teaching job materialised.

3

A PROTEST ON POLLING DAY

'Do you know, Annie, three states have already won the vote for women!' It was October, and Molly and Annie were on their way to a meeting of the Women's Suffrage Association in Houston Street, where Mrs Elizabeth Cady Stanton – one of the pioneers of women's suffrage, and now over eighty years of age – would deliver a lecture entitled 'How Western Women Won the Vote'. It was hard to believe that this woman had been working to get women the vote since 1848!

Annie had only just made it home in time to have something quick to eat before going to the meeting with Molly. Tonight she would enrol as a member of the association.

'Nebraska women don't have the vote, I

know,' she replied. 'Although Mike says that if Jennings Bryan gets in, he would favour it.'

'Well, I for one would not vote for him if he didn't,' said Molly. 'Wyoming, Utah and now Colorado have all granted women the vote, so it would be a poor show if he didn't try to secure it for Nebraska women at least.'

They arrived just in time to find seats, as the hall was crowded, mostly with women, but a fair handful of men were present too. Annie had hoped Mike might be there but he was working so hard on the election campaign that it was unlikely he would be. She was pleased that Mike was so supportive of the association. Most men were not, she knew. When she had mentioned the meeting in the lunch room at work, she had drawn a blank stare from most of her colleagues. Mr Lewis from Carpets, who made use of any opportunity to get to speak with Miss Sarah Waters and had just dropped in on the pretext of delivering her a note, stopped and stared at Annie in shock.

'I didn't think you were that sort of

person,' he said, looking at her as if she were a criminal.

Only Susan Wilcox murmured timidly, 'Sounds like a fine idea to me...' Her voice faded out for want of encouragement.

Now, as she looked around, she wondered if she would see anyone from work, but she didn't. However, to her great surprise she spotted Alice Rodgers, whom she had worked with in her first job at the Phoenix Laundry before it burned down four years before. She determined to have a word with her later.

It was an entertaining evening. Mrs Cady Stanton, for all that she had to be assisted to the platform, was a forceful speaker.

'When we started this association, back in '69, we thought it was only a matter of time before every woman in the United States would have the right to vote,' she began. 'We had just seen the Territory of Wyoming allow women to vote. And what's more, they held on to it, and when the time came for them to join the Union in 1890, they refused to come in unless their women could hold on to that privilege. In 1870, we saw the women of Utah get the vote, and they have held on to it. Finally, only a few years ago, they were joined by Colorado.'

Annie and Molly were fascinated by the small, stout, white-haired old lady who was still so full of passion for the campaign to enable women to take, as she put it, 'their rightful place in society'.

Mrs Cady Stanton then introduced her daughter Harriot, who, she said, lived with her husband and daughter in England, but who would speak about the experiences of women suffragists in that country.

A handsome woman stood up to speak and soon had them transfixed with tales of how hard women worked for the vote in England. There they were called 'suffragettes', she explained, and they went to all sorts of extremes to fight for their cause.

'You must do what men do when they want to get a law passed,' she urged them.

'You must lobby those who make the laws and you must get out there and march for what you believe in.' The actions of British suffragettes, she said, were an example of the lengths to which women would go to fight for this most worthy and noble of causes.

Loud cheers greeted her speech, and when the meeting ended the audience trooped out on a wave of enthusiasm and resolve.

Waiting in line to enrol, Annie bumped right into Alice Rodgers and they greeted each other with delight.

'I'd heard you'd gone to the West,' said Alice. 'Sophia told me, but I did not know of your return. It's no surprise to me that you are joining up too. Remember when we worked in the laundry how keen you were on getting us into the trade union?'

They laughed, recalling the lunchtime meetings in the cloakroom before the horror of the fire overtook them, causing such tragic loss of life. They looked at each other, silent for a moment as they relived the shared experience.

Alice told Annie that she was now working as supervisor in a large steam laundry on East Fourteenth Street, and was also an active member of the Laundry Workers' Union. 'I've learned my lesson the hard way,' she said.

Annie also learned from Alice that her friend Sophia Rostov, whom she had thought was still nursing in Bellevue Hospital, had left it, and, along with a colleague, had started up a home for abandoned children in the Lower East Side.

'Well, that explains why I have not heard a word from her since I returned to New York,' she said. 'I wrote to her at the hospital but received no reply and her family have moved away from Orchard Street.'

Alice was able to tell her where Sophia now worked and Annie resolved to contact her friend as soon as possible. Parting from Alice with promises to meet soon, she and Molly set off home, delighted with the evening's entertainment and full of plans to further their cause in every way they could.

It was some time, however, before Annie got an opportunity to catch up with Sophia, as with little over a month to go to the presidential election every spare moment she had was now given over to helping Mike with the campaign.

While hope abounded among all his supporters that William Jennings Bryan would win the campaign for the Democrats, it was not at all as easy to predict as President Cleveland's victory four years previously had been. To everyone's surprise, Bryan, the people's hero, had not been a great success in New York.

Much to Mike's chagrin, the rally in Madison Square Gardens had been described as a 'fiasco' by the *New York Herald* and their candidate had lost ground rapidly in the following weeks. In contrast, the Republican's candidate, Mr McKinley, was gaining in popularity all the time. Even in Nebraska, Bryan's own state, Mike told Annie, no one could be sure if William Jennings Bryan could carry the day against the Republicans.

'If the man can't carry his own people after all he did for them,' said Father, puffing worriedly on his pipe, 'there isn't much anyone can do for him.'

Mike wouldn't hear of such talk, however, and merely redoubled his efforts. Each evening, as soon as Annie was finished work, she and Molly would join Mike and Tom at Tammany Hall and throw themselves into electioneering.

Assisting in the putting together of the election literature and forming teams to go out and distribute it, as well as making tea for the ever-increasing hordes of workers, were only some of the tasks she and Molly undertook every night.

Annie enjoyed this opportunity to see Mike so regularly and entered with gusto into the excitement of the campaign. No matter how hard or how late they all worked, there was always the quiet stroll home together to look forward to. Hand in hand, they would walk slowly, relishing the opportunity to be alone together. Mike's embrace as they parted each evening was so loving that, no matter how late it was or how exhausted she felt, Annie sailed up those four flights of stairs as if walking on air.

Tom and Molly, too, appeared to be happy together and spent much time planning their future – where they would live and the date they would wed. Often, as the four young people walked home at night, snatches of Tom and Molly's lively exchanges would escape, like sparks in the night air, and float back to Annie and Mike, who, wrapped up in their own little world, were oblivious to anyone else's problems or plans.

It was in the week prior to the election that Molly and Annie devised a daring plan.

A recent newsletter of the Suffrage Association had described in detail some of the exploits carried out by more militant members in the far West.

Reading through it, a thought struck Annie. 'Molly, listen to this.' Then she read out a description of how, prior to gaining the vote in Colorado in '93, some women had made so bold as to present themselves at the polling booths in an attempt to vote in a federal election. For their pains, they were hurried away by the authorities and locked up in prison for the night.

'Why don't we do it too, Molly?' said Annie excitedly. 'What can they do to punish us? It's not a hanging offence!'

'You mean, we should just go to the polls to vote? Hmmm ... well, why not? What would Tom and Mike think, I wonder?'

'Let's not tell them. They'd only try and stop us. We must do it, Molly, we must! It's the best way to show how foolish it is not to let us vote – by just forcing them to stop us. Oh, let's do it!'

Annie soon infected Molly with her enthusiasm for this escapade and they lay awake half the night planning how they would go about it. Would they carry it out alone or invite some other members of the association to come along? Would they dress up as men in order to gain entry? Could they actually succeed in voting?

'We'll do it by ourselves because we will have more chance of getting away with it. If there are too many of us, the people at the booth will suspect there is something going on, and we won't even be able to gain entrance, never mind vote,' Molly pointed out.

'Perhaps we could pretend that we had a message for someone in the building,' Annie suggested. 'An urgent message. Then they would have to let us in.'

Gradually, the plan took shape, and eventually, when polling day dawned, the two girls were up very early. They had to act before Annie went to work, as the polls would close at five o'clock in the afternoon, before she could leave the store. Luckily, they opened at 6 am. Molly was not pressed for time, as she had begun her new job in the kindergarten school and did not start until nine o'clock each morning.

Dressed in their Sunday best, they made straight for the nearest polling office at an early hour. Their strategy was that, if they were challenged at the entrance, they would present a letter which they would say had to be personally delivered to the office's supervisor. If they gained entrance, they would have to rely on their wits from then on. If they didn't, they would go on to the next polling office and the next, continuing until they succeeded.

Nervous, but determined to take this opportunity to strike their own blow for women's freedom to vote, the two girls approached the entrance. Not many people were out to vote at this hour, and certainly there were no women accompanying the handful of men who were around. That was a pity, as they would now attract more attention. If there had been some couples, they could, perhaps, have attached themselves discreetly to someone and managed to gain entrance without being spotted.

'What can I do for you, ladies?' boomed the usher, smiling broadly at the spectacle of two fashionable young ladies out and about at this early hour of the day.

This was their chance. Swallowing hard, Annie stepped forward and, with a very serious expression, said earnestly, 'It is most important, sir, that I have a word with the supervisor inside. I have an urgent message for him.'

The official's expression changed to one of polite deference. He had no reason, after all, to doubt the word of two such well-dressed young women.

'Well, if you would just wait a moment...' he began. These were words they didn't wish to hear and Molly interjected quickly: 'We would not wish to fetch the gentleman from his work but if you would kindly tell us where to go, we shall not be a minute, and be off out of your way.'

The official looked doubtful and scratched his head. He should fetch the supervisor, or go and deliver this 'urgent message' himself, but then he was on door duty, wasn't he, and would be in right hot water should any villains gain access to the building.

Finally he said, 'Okay then, young ladies,

down to the end of that corridor and the first door on your right – you can follow those gentlemen going to place their vote – and be quick about it.'

The girls could hardly believe their luck. Concealing their jubilance, they bowed their heads demurely and proceeded quickly in the direction indicated. As they reached the door, they looked at each other. Molly nodded and, hearts thumping, they entered the room.

They didn't attract undue attention as they followed closely in the wake of two or three gentlemen who were about to cast their votes. As they stood in line with the men who were waiting to approach the supervisor, they glanced around them quickly and spotted the large steel box where those who had filled in the name of their choice were placing their voting slips. As the gentleman in front of them received his voting paper from the supervisor, they suddenly made a dash for it and succeeded in putting slips of paper with the name 'William Jennings

Bryan' written on them in large lettering into the box before the startled officials could step forward to stop them.

'Women must have the right to vote!' Annie declared loudly, while inside she was nearly fainting from fright.

All hell broke loose. The man at the door of the room sounded a whistle, banging the door shut as he did so. Voters stood back, astounded. The girls found themselves being forcefully ushered into an adjoining room and surrounded by a group of outraged officials.

'What do you think you're doing?'

'How dare you enter this building!'

'How did you get in here?'

'Women cannot vote!'

'Who put you up to this?'

Abuse rained down on them from all sides and, confused and intimidated, they clung together in the centre of it all. 'Women in Wyoming, Utah and Colorado can vote,' ventured Molly, determined to make her contribution.

Suddenly, one of the men laughed and it must have been infectious, because next thing the girls knew, they were surrounded by a whole circle of men, laughing uproariously and pointing at them with derision. Humiliated by this outburst, but relieved – they had anticipated prison at the very least – they waited until it had all subsided and then asked with exaggerated politeness if they might leave.

There was another frightening moment when the supervisor said, half-seriously, 'If you were men, you'd be thrown in prison for this jape,' to which Annie couldn't help retorting, 'If we were men, we could vote.'

However, time was passing, and outside, the corridor was full of waiting men wondering what the delay was. The supervisor, having delivered a short, sharp lecture, told them to be off 'and if I ever find you up to these tricks again, it will be the Tombs Prison for you.'

Shaken but triumphant, Annie and Molly, released at last, hugged each other gleefully.

They had made their point.

This early-morning adventure on polling day was soon forgotten, however, in the wake of the election, when it emerged that William Jennings Bryan was not going to be the victor. Mike and Tom were inconsolable and not likely to be distracted by the girls' exploits. Mr McKinley, it appeared, was going to top the polls and win by a great majority.

'The landslide has completely swept the country north of the Virginian line, from the Atlantic almost to the Rocky Mountains,' read Mike ruefully from the *New York Herald*.

Two days later, it was all over. Their hero had been well and truly beaten and the Republicans were in government. Disconsolate, Annie and Molly joined the subdued crowds at Tammany Hall to clear away all vestiges of such a humiliating defeat. Their own humiliation seemed very minor by comparison and they decided to save their tale for another day.

But in their hearts they hoarded the delicious secret that they, Annie Moore and

Molly O'Byrne, had been the only two women in the whole of New York State – indeed in most states – to have claimed their vote on polling day.

4

SOPHIA AND THE BRIGHT ANGELS

Dear Annie, wrote Carl in his large, old-fashioned, slanty handwriting. He must have got her address from Gertrude, Annie reflected, with a stab of guilt. It was now early December and, despite promising to do so, she had not written to Carl once since returning to New York. She had thought of him many times, but did not really know what to write. If she wrote, she would perhaps only encourage him in this notion that he loved her.

Another reason why she had not written to him was that she had never got around to telling Mike about Carl. She feared it might sound as if she harboured feelings for him. But then, she did harbour some feelings for him. Of course she did: they had been tremendous friends. Why, oh why, she thought as she settled down with the letter, did life have to be so confusing?

I guess there isn't much point in waiting any longer for a letter from you, so here's one from me just to keep you posted so to speak. I've heard news of you from Trudie, which is only second-best, but it seems you are well and happy and having a rare ole time which makes me happy.

Life here goes on as ever, with very little happening and no Irish redheads shooting arrows at me from way out east. Just as well, I suppose as I'm gonna get out of this place before long. Haven't told the folks yet, but I'll be headin' off to join a bunch of folk down in Arizona. They think there's goin' to be a war in Cuba sometime soon, on account of all the trouble there, and they aim on trainin' a bunch of us to be ready to join up if that happens. Myself, I'm not so sure it will, but it can't hurt just headin' off and havin' a go.

I thought to come and visit you in New York before that, but I reckon I won't be doin' that now. I'll be in touch, though. If you get this before Thanksgiving you might reply, but I'll be headin' off soon after, as I don't want to get snowed in here for another winter.

You take care now.

Yours ever

Carl

Tears pricked Annie's eyes. She felt badly. The least she could have done was write and tell him how she was. But now he was heading off to fight some stupid war that might not even happen, although now she thought of it, Mike had many times spoken of the possibility of a Spanish-American war. Something to do with the way Spain was treating the people in Cuba, or something. But why a war?

It was too late to write to Carl now. It was almost two weeks since Thanksgiving, and no doubt he would have left for Arizona already.

Annie sighed, put the letter down and stared into space. Her thoughts turned to Mike. He had been very disillusioned over the presidential election, as had a lot of young Democrats. He had turned his attention to his work in recent weeks and she knew he was not happy.

It was bad luck, too, that Mike's boss, Mr Bartholomew Gibson, was active in the City Vigilance League and had frowned on Mike's political activities all along. But now that the election was over, he had given Mike to understand he would have to make a choice: his job or politics. With the Democrats now in real disarray, and an air of disillusionment rife, Mike felt he had no choice but to hold on to his job. Even though he hadn't complained, Annie knew deep down that he had lost heart. In his head, he knew it was the right decision to stay in his job, but his heart would always be in political action.

'I know I could make good at this work and open my own business as a tailor eventually,' he told Annie. 'I want to do so much more in politics, but I don't dare, if I want to hold on to my job.'

Deprived of that solace, Mike threw himself into his work and Annie fretted for him.

As Christmas approached, however, life took on a brighter aspect – for Annie, at least. A. & T. Stewart's was a refuge from the dark days, with their threatening skies and freezing-cold temperatures. Each morning as Annie approached the store, her heart lifted at the sight of the fairy-tale Christmas windows. She and Molly had had great fun one Sunday when they brought young Patrick to see them. He was enthralled and banged on the windows with his tiny gloved fists, shouting 'Father Christmas, Father Christmas, please come to my house.'

The Christmas season had begun at A. & T. Stewart's as early as the first week in December. The premises was ablaze with electric lights, and Christmas decorations festooned every inch of the store. The employees were very busy, as the store extended its opening hours every evening in the run-up to Christmas. Annie found herself obliged to work late two or three evenings a week.

While Molly would go home to Brooklyn for the Christmas holidays as soon as her kindergarten closed, Annie would be working right up to Christmas Eve. She longed for Christmas Day, which she would spend with her family. Mike, who had no family in America – they had all remained in Ireland – would join them too.

It was after nine o'clock when Annie left the store one evening about a week before Christmas. She was tired to her bones. Molly had left that day for Brooklyn and, while she didn't relish going back to an empty flat, she knew she really needed just to crawl into bed and have a good, sound sleep. All this extra work was catching up with her and she didn't want to be too worn out to enjoy Christmas. Mike was working late, too, she knew, for the tailoring business was also subject to the Christmas rush. Never mind, only one more week until Christmas, when they would have two whole days to enjoy each other's company. He had promised to take her skating in Central Park on St Stephen's Day.

Thinking about this and humming softly to herself, she nearly tripped over the scarecrow figure of a young girl who thrust a box under her nose, just outside the store.

'Please, miss, spare a dime for a girl as can't afford to buy nowt for Christmas.'

Annie looked at the wizened face and experienced a sudden shock of recognition.

'Peggy!' she exclaimed. 'Peggy Sullivan, it is you, isn't it?'

The girl looked startled out of her wits and made to dart away but Annie had her by the arm. It was indeed Peggy, who had worked as the scullery maid in the Van der Leutens' home when Annie had worked there as parlour maid. What in heaven's name was she doing, begging outside A. & T. Stewart's on this cold, frosty night, Annie wondered.

'Miss Annie,' she stammered, 'I'm ever so sorry, I didn't know you at all.' She looked up at Annie in a combination of fear and wonder, and wriggled with embarrassment at the scrutiny she was receiving.

'Peggy, what are you doing here? Have you no place to go?' Annie could scarcely contain her dismay. Peggy looked a fright. Her clothes were ragged and torn, her hair unbrushed, her feet bare, and she looked even more underfed and frail than she had when Annie had last seen her, over two years before.

Judging it unwise to stand outside the store talking to this poor urchin for any longer, Annie took her arm, marched her off without waiting for an answer and propelled her along the street. She had no idea what she was going to do with Peggy.

The whole story emerged later, when, reluctant to enter any respectable tea shop with Peggy in tow, Annie saw nothing for it but to bring her home with her for the night. The girl's teeth were chattering with the cold, and Annie could get no sense out of her until she had her wrapped in a comforter, sipping a glass of hot chocolate. She had hastily lit the stove as soon as they came in and it was just beginning to throw out a bit of warmth when Peggy, perhaps encouraged by the hot drink and the promise of a warm bed, at last began to talk.

'You see, I lost me job at the Van der Leutens' a year back now,' she began. ''Twas how I had one of me turns when I was in the kitchen and knocked a pot off of the stove. Cook got scalded and the Mistress gave me me walkin' papers and said on no account to come back ever again.'

While sympathetic, Annie could barely conceal a smile at the scene this conjured up in her mind. Peggy had finally taken a 'turn' too many. The combined wrath of the Mistress and Cook must have been something to behold. Poor Peggy.

'What did you do then?' she asked, knowing Peggy had a family and wondering how she had come to be in this state.

'Well, see, me Ma threw me out then, for I was bringin' in nowt and she needed the money, what with the bairns to look after and me Pa gone...'

'And then...?' prompted Annie, at last beginning to understand. Poor Peggy would have found it very hard to get another job.

'Then, not havin' a character nor nothin' – the Mistress refused to give me one, she said I was worse than useless anyway – I went to the Sisters in St Aloysius. They used to let me have a bed for the night. I wanted to work but I couldn't get in any place. I didn't want to beg, ever, but it's how I had to in the end.' She gulped tearfully and bowed her head, unable to go on.

Silence fell. Annie was in a quandary. Whatever could she do with Peggy? She couldn't keep her here. Molly would be back after Christmas and she didn't know where else the poor child could go. Somehow, though, it had suddenly become her responsibility.

'You can stay here for tonight anyway, Peggy, and we'll talk again in the morning,' she said, preparing a bed for the girl on the settle beside the fire, which was now burning brightly.

In bed she tossed and turned, trying to come up with a solution. There must be some way to help Peggy. Suddenly it came to her. Hadn't Alice Rodgers said that Sophia was running some kind of refuge for abandoned children somewhere in the Lower East Side? Luckily she had given her the address. Annie hoped she could find it. She had still not had time to contact her friend. Now the opportunity to do so had fallen into her lap. In fact, she really had no choice. She would go and see Sophia first thing the next day. She had a couple of hours off in the morning, as she was due to work late again the following evening. Yes, she was sure Sophia could have some solution to Peggy's problems.

She rose early the next morning and got Peggy in and out of the bathroom before any of the other tenants were about. She particularly did not want the landlady to catch sight of Peggy or there would be questions asked. She managed to find some clothes that, although they were too large, didn't look too bad on the girl. Indeed, by the time they were ready to leave, she looked a million times better than she had the night before. Poor Peggy. She had slept like the dead and looked much refreshed. It was as if finding someone she knew to look after her had been a great relief to her spirit.

As they crept out the front door and set off, Annie did not know what she would say to Sophia. She did not even know if Sophia would still be at this address. God knows what she would do with Peggy if Sophia was unable to help her.

Taking a trolley-car, it was not too long before they reached the area Annie was looking for. After a further ten minutes' walk, they found the house, down at the end of Market Street towards the East River – one of the poorest districts in the whole of New York, as Annie knew well. Even Monroe Street, where her family had lived for so long in cramped conditions, was a lot more salubrious than this.

The house she was looking for was the corner house on the block with an entrance at the side, reached by a narrow laneway. On a crude wooden sign nailed to the wall, the words 'Bright Angel Refuge' were painted. Behind the tall, cast-iron gates, Annie could see a small courtyard, which to her surprise was filled with colourful plants in pots and a small, puny tree growing against the high wall. Humble it may have been, but such a sight in the centre of one of the most densely populated areas of New York was extra-ordinary. Any kind of yard was a luxury in these parts, but this little space, catching narrow beams of early-morning winter sun, almost had the air of a garden. She pulled a rope and a bell clanged inside the courtyard.

'I'll be right there,' called a light, musical voice Annie knew and loved.

Sophia Rostov, as vivacious and fleet-footed as ever, came running to the gate, a large iron key in her hand. Seeing Annie, her dark brown eyes lit up.

'Annie! Annie!' she cried, tussling im-patiently with the lock. 'How wonderful! However did you find me?'

The two old friends embraced warmly, Sophia exclaiming over her friend's fashionable attire and glowing looks.

'I only heard recently you were back from the West. I had hoped you would be in touch, because I had no way of contacting you since your family left Monroe Street,' she said.

'And it was the same for me since your family left Orchard Street,' replied Annie. 'But I got this address from Alice Rodgers a while back. Remember Alice from the laundry? Thank God you're still here. I had meant to come sooner, but...' Annie hesitated and then drew Peggy forward. The girl looked silently from one friend to the other, her eyes round with hope.

Immediately, Sophia took charge of the situation, ushering them both into a basement kitchen and pouring large, steaming beakers of coffee.

'Have some bread and butter with it,' she urged Peggy gently, and the young girl needed no second bidding. Then Sophia drew Annie out through a dark passageway and into a tiny cubbyhole, which had been ingeniously converted into an office.

Over the next twenty minutes, Annie heard a remarkable story. Annie had first met Sophia Rostov in the Phoenix Laundry and they had become firm friends. Sophia had gone on to train as a nurse at Bellevue Hospital and had qualified a year previously. Being surrounded by illness and deprivation of all kinds in the hospital upset the soft-hearted Sophia. She and her friend, fellow nurse Jenny Foster, often talked about it and wished they could do something to help the many needy people who passed through the hospital doors – especially the children, many of whom were abandoned and ill-treated.

'One night,' Sophia confided, 'we saw a shocking sight. I had been called out to a house nearby with one of the doctors to attend a birth. We heard it was going to be a difficult one, so Jenny came along too.

'On the top floor of a house quite near here, we found the woman lying on a mattress on the floor in a small room with four children – all little ones – crawling about her. One of the neighbours had called to the hospital for help. Her husband, it seemed, had died of TB only weeks before and now, as well as being about to give birth, she was also very ill with the disease.

'She had no strength left and expired as soon as we had delivered the baby. The room was cold and dirty, the children filthy, hungry and crying miserably. But when she passed away, there was this sudden, terrible silence for a few moments, as if each one of those little souls knew their mother was gone. Within the space of an hour, there were five of them, and both parents dead.'

Annie was aghast. 'What happened to them?' she asked.

'I don't know. They were taken into care somewhere, but after that night Jenny and I knew we would have to do something to prevent that kind of thing from happening. We didn't know what to do and had to really think about it.'

The two young nurses soon formed a plan to open a refuge where they could look after abandoned children until homes could be found for them. But they needed funding. First they managed to interest a Russian doctor – a friend of Sophia's brother Josef – in the project. He would help them establish the home, provided they were able to come up with suitable accommodation.

It seemed an impossible task. The girls used every minute of their spare time raising funds and looking for a place. They received quite a bit of support from the hospital, who thought it was a fine idea.

'Raising the money to get it going was the most difficult part,' said Sophia. 'The Society for Poor and Destitute Families has been our main support – they own this house – and it is through them mainly that the children come here. Sometimes, of course, they just arrive, or get left at the gate and we have to manage as best we can.'

Annie then told Sophia Peggy's story, adding, 'I do not expect that you will be able to take her in, but even if you could give her a bed at night for a little while in return for some help around the place, I would be very grateful. She could be a great help – she just needs someone to watch her and tell her what to do.'

'I'll gladly take her, Annie. I could well do with the help, as Jenny is not here all the time. Now, let me show you both around.'

Annie left Bright Angel Refuge an hour later, feeling deeply relieved about Peggy and both moved and impressed by her friend's work. The small premises comprised a dormitory, a schoolroom and the large basement kitchen. It was brightly painted and decorated and a large stove ensured it was also warm. Although it was only half past seven in the morning, it housed twelve or so little 'bright angels', who were wide awake and in the process of being dressed and fed. Most were little ones of about three or four and there were a few older ones. But it was the air of good cheer that made the most favourable impression on Annie: good cheer in the face of great adversity.

Lost in thoughts of her friend's courage and resourcefulness, she was jolted back to reality on being summoned to Miss Gilroy's office later that afternoon. The minute she entered the room, she felt the chill of disapproval.

'It has come to my attention, Miss Moore, that you were seen talking to a tramp outside the front entrance last evening,' she said sternly.

'I … you see…' Annie began, but was instantly silenced by Miss Gilroy's uplifted hand.

'It is not my business whom you mix with when not at work here, Miss Moore, as long as you do not flaunt your undesirable connections in full view of the store. You were seen accompanying this person along the street as if you were old friends. I just wish to warn you that we do not tolerate that sort of thing here at A. & T. Stewart's, so please do not be seen in such a situation again. Thank you – you may go back to work now.'

With not the least opportunity to explain

herself, Annie was dismissed and found herself staring at a closed door. Boiling with indignation, she returned downstairs. How unjust and unfair this woman's judgement had been. Suddenly the bright lights of A. & T. Stewart's seemed tawdry and meaningless, her work there paltry and unworthy. The spell had been broken. She could only think of the genuine warmth and sincerity with which Sophia had taken Peggy in and of the smiling faces of the children eating breakfast when she left.

5

CHANGES AND PARTINGS

Christmas Day dawned bitterly cold but sunny. Heavy snow had fallen over the previous few days, making it almost treacherous to venture out on the streets. That, however, did not deter Annie, Norah and Charlie from making the journey on foot to the Moores' apartment just off Delancey Street, where they were all to spend the day together.

Having worked until very late the night before, Annie had returned to Cherry Street to stay with her aunt and uncle for the Christmas break, and all three were in high spirits. They had been to early Mass and now, laden with Christmas gifts for the family, they carefully picked their way through the snowy streets.

'Happy Christmas, happy Christmas!' They were greeted with cries of delight by Philip and little Patrick, who had been watching out for their arrival and pelted them with snow-balls the minute they appeared. Grown far beyond these childish antics and quite the young man about town, Anthony soon came to their rescue, hurrying them inside out of the cold.

How wonderful it was to be here with her family for Christmas, Annie thought, looking around in admiration at the cheerfully decorated apartment. She could not help comparing it to their previous home in Monroe Street and noting that here at last there was enough space for the family, and even for a proper Christmas tree this year.

Her parents had come up in the world a little and now at last had something to show for their years of hard work, Annie reflected with satisfaction. Indeed, they still had three of their six children to provide for, although Philip would soon be at an age to go out into the world and fend for himself. She wondered again about their plans to go off to Arizona, and whether it was wise. She thought briefly of Carl and the coincidence of his being there now. He would be surprised to find out that her family planned on going out to Arizona too, she thought.

Tom arrived with Mike in tow shortly afterwards and then the festivities began in earnest. Mother had surpassed herself. First she served clam chowder, which warmed them all up. Uncle Charlie had come up trumps with a fine creel of clams from the

Fulton Fish Market, where he worked. This was followed by roast goose with all the trimmings; this evoked memories of Christmases back in Cork, where, no matter how strained finances were, they were always sure of a goose for the Christmas.

Auntie North had made her mouth-watering Christmas pudding, which, decorated with a sprig of holly, was presented with great fanfare. Even baby Elizabeth, sitting on Annie's lap, clapped her pudgy little hands with delight at the sight of it.

'Well 'tis glad I am to have my family around me this Christmas day, and especially our dear Annie, who was sorely missed these past two years.'

Father, his usual gruff voice softened on this happy occasion, lifted his glass of port in a toast to his eldest daughter. This brought a 'Hear, hear' from all around the table and an especially heartfelt one from Mike, whose eyes rested with love and affection on the young woman at his side.

After dinner, they settled down to a grand

session of songs and storytelling around the stove. Uncle Charlie accompanied the singing on his banjo and they sang all the Irish songs they remembered. Annie regaled them with tales of her adventures in Nebraska and then sang 'She is Far from the Land', which Mike had never heard her sing before.

Tom treated them to a dramatic recitation of 'The Midnight Ride of Paul Revere', which tells of this brave rebel's frenzied gallop to alert the populace of the advance of the British troops under cover of night:

Listen my children and you shall hear
Of the midnight ride of Paul Revere...
On the eighteenth of April in Seventy-Five;
Hardly a man is now alive
Who remembers that famous day and year.

His audience listened with rapt attention as he evoked the terrible happenings of that fateful night. When he came to:

A moment only he feels the spell
Of the place and the hour and the secret dread
Of the lonely belfry and the dead;
For suddenly all his thoughts are bent
On a shadowy something far away,
Where the river widens to meet the bay,
A line of black that bends and floats
On the rising tide like a bridge of boats

little Patrick jumped into his father's lap with a squeal of terror and the great performance had to be abandoned until he had been soothed.

When it was Mike's turn, harmony was restored with his rendering of 'Beautiful Dreamer' in a rich baritone voice. He made Annie blush by gazing straight at her throughout.

It had been a perfect day and Annie knew that it would remain with her forever. She regretted only that dear Molly could not have been with them. However, seeing as she would soon marry Tom, it was only fair that she stay with her own family in Brooklyn this Christmas. She thought too of Ellie, Dan and the children, snug and happy in their grand new frame-house on the prairie. Finally, as her eyes rested on the youngest, treasured member of her family, baby Elizabeth, she thought of the Bright Angel Refuge and the children who had sought shelter there and wondered what kind of Christmas her friend Sophia was having.

Annie's opportunity to tell Mike about the strange circumstances of her reunion with Sophia did not come until the next day. The snow held off again, allowing them to join the crowds who took to the skating rink in Central Park. Mike, already skilled at the sport, led a more tentative Annie around the rink until eventually she was gliding along at his side with the confidence of a born skater.

'You've got roses in your cheeks,' Mike teased as they strolled homewards later that afternoon, well pleased with their outing. They were to rejoin the family at Cherry Street, where Auntie Norah had promised high tea to all comers.

Glad to have the opportunity to talk alone with him, Annie told Mike all about her adventure with Peggy the previous week and about its consequences. While obviously impressed by Sophia's enterprise, Mike declared himself not surprised by the reaction of Miss Gilroy at A. & T. Stewart's.

'It's only those with money and riches that impress people like her,' he declared with passion. 'Little they care for the Peggys of this world. If they can't afford to buy at A. & T. Stewart's, they don't count.'

'I didn't realise that when I went to work for them,' replied Annie. 'It is a good place to work and I suppose I was so impressed with it all. I should have heeded you at the beginning. Anyway, I plan to leave in a couple of weeks and take the teaching job at St Margaret's. They wrote to me saying that they are expecting me from the beginning of the term.

'Somehow, meeting Sophia again and seeing her with those poor mites brought me to my senses. I plan to spend a lot of time helping her out. Maybe Molly might help too, because even though Sophia's friend Jenny is there some of the time, she mostly has to look after the place all on her own.'

'You will be a great success at the teaching, Annie, I'm sure of it. As for Sophia, I may be able to help out there. Mr Gibson is a member of a Benevolent Society and I am sure he would be able to spare some funds towards such a good cause.'

Annie felt so much better now that she had confided in Mike and had come to the decision to leave A. & T. Stewart's. She had had some fun there and it had been good experience, but her heart was no longer in it. She had not spent that year studying to be a teacher in Lincoln only to languish behind the Ladies' Fashions counter in A. & T. Stewart's. She was ready now for a real challenge.

Next day, Annie was back at work. The sales had begun and she was run off her feet. Nonetheless, she found time to visit Miss Gilroy's office and give in her notice. Apart from remarking that her timing for doing so was poor, Miss Gilroy said little, except that A. & T. Stewart's would be sorry to lose her. The woman regretted her hasty words to Annie before Christmas and felt that this was the real reason the girl was leaving. Perhaps there had been a reasonable explanation for what had happened. Miss Moore was a bright girl, after all, and Miss Gilroy had nothing but good reports about her work.

'I am sorry to leave during the sales, Miss Gilroy, but I am taking up a teaching post and I have to start on the first day of term,' Annie explained.

Miss Gilroy was surprised. Teaching, was it? Well now, Miss Moore *was* a dark horse.

But not being the most generous of people, she made no comment. 'I see,' was all she said.

Annie's final two weeks at the store were the busiest since she had come to work there. There were late-night openings for the sales and crowds of shoppers filled the store each day from early morning until late in the evening. However, she at least profited from the opportunity to buy some good boots and serviceable skirts and shirtwaists for herself at keen prices. Not only did she get the sale reduction but there was a further percentage off for staff members. She knew that on an assistant teacher's salary there would be little hope of buying good-quality clothes for some time to come.

Molly's return after her Christmas break was a welcome event and the two friends found time to catch up on news late at night on Annie's return from work. Molly was agog to hear about Peggy and the meeting with Sophia. As Annie knew she would, she instantly agreed to help out at Bright Angel Refuge.

'To tell the truth, Moll, if I hadn't agreed to take up this teaching job, and if I could earn a living at the refuge, I would have thrown in my lot with Sophia myself,' Annie confided.

'You'll see, Annie, we'll be able to help her out a lot. Perhaps we could organise an event to raise money for them. I'll ask Tom about it. He might have some ideas.'

Sunday being the first free day Annie had that week, she brought Molly around to the refuge. Sophia was delighted to see them both again and Molly was as impressed as Annie at the work she was doing.

But the real surprise was Peggy. She looked a different person to the sad ragamuffin Annie had brought there two weeks previously. Clad in a respectable work dress covered by a gleaming white apron, her hair tied back neatly, Peggy was transformed. Her expression, too, was brighter and happier and she was able to meet Annie's eyes without shame or fear.

'Peggy is a great help.' Sophia praised the girl warmly. 'She gets the little ones ready in the mornings and sees to their breakfast as well as doing many other tasks. I am so happy to have her here.' Although she didn't say a word, Peggy's eyes lit up at this praise and Annie could see that she had already formed a warm attachment to Sophia.

They spent a delightful afternoon there, and on this occasion there was plenty of time to see how the refuge worked and what their problems were. Annie and Molly were introduced to all the children over tea, and once the meal was over the two women played with them for an hour or so. Sophia was genuinely pleased when they offered to help her as often as they could.

'But you are both working,' she said, looking earnestly from one to the other. 'How can you find time...?'

Having reassured their friend, they sat down and worked out a timetable which would allow Sophia to count on their help and even manage to grasp a little free time of her own. They had been shocked to hear that she had not been able to visit her family over the Christmas holidays as there was no one to look after her own little extended family of bright angels.

'But I thought you had someone else here working with you ... your friend, Jenny?' Annie asked.

'Jenny helps when she can but she is an only daughter in her family and has to spend a lot of time with her mother, who is ill,' Sophia explained.

Annie's sympathy for her friend deepened and she was heartily glad they had been reunited. On the way home, she and Molly discussed ways of helping her.

At last the day came for Annie to start her new job as an assistant teacher at St Margaret's School. Recalling her first day working at the little twenty-five-pupil prairie school in Kimball two years previously, she couldn't help comparing it with this large, modern school in the Lower East Side of New York City, which catered for several hundred children from the surrounding districts.

'Welcome to St Margaret's, Miss Moore.' The principal, Sister O'Keeffe, warmly greeted the new young assistant teacher standing in her office.

'Now, for the first while we'll put you with Miss Donnelly and the little ones,' she explained. 'Let me show you where to go.'

Annie soon settled in. She became first

assistant to the infant teacher Miss Donnelly in the girls' section and, with her, took charge of the sixty or so youngest girls in the school. She was to be paid a salary of five hundred dollars a year.

Each day started with the Pledge of Allegiance. Even though most of the children in the school were from immigrant families and could speak little or no English, they were quickly given to understand that saluting the American flag in assembly every morning was one of the most important moments of the day. Annie smiled to see some of the tiny ones make this important gesture with solemn faces, even though they had no idea what they were doing. Riveted, they would watch an older boy or girl proudly hold up the national flag at the head of the hall for all to see.

In class, Annie found she was expected to be very strict and 'keeping order' was to be high on her list of priorities. They were fortunate, Miss Donnelly told her, in being one of the few schools in the district to have a rooftop playground where the children ate lunch and took recreation in all weathers. Having somewhere to let off steam on occasion made them easier to handle in class.

One of the most important tasks was to teach the children how to speak English. It was only by mastering this language that the immigrant children would be able to make progress in school and so move on into the world of work.

Many of the children were Irish, Annie noticed, but those who were relatively recently arrived in America were almost as much at a loss in communicating as those who spoke Russian, German or Italian. Many of them did not make good progress, though, and Annie found there were one or two older children in her class who were being held back with the younger ones because of their inability to speak English. These children, ashamed of lagging behind with the 'babies', could cause trouble from time to time and, after a week or two at her new post, Annie understood the necessity of 'keeping order'.

All in all, however, she enjoyed her work, happy to rediscover the satisfaction she had found in teaching when she had first started in Nebraska. She was grateful, too, to have more time of her own, as school finished at three o'clock each afternoon. Molly was finished around the same time and often the two of them would meet and head straight off to the refuge to help Sophia with the 'angels', as they called them.

Once a week, she and Mike would take tea together at one of the smart new tearooms near where he worked, if he could get off in good time. Annie longed for these occasions, and as soon as she saw her tall, handsome boyfriend swing through the door to join her, she would think how happy she was nowadays and how everything had come right, as she had always known it would.

It came as quite a shock, then, when one day in early March she arrived home from school to find her younger brother Philip pacing up and down outside the house where she lived on St Mark's Place.

'Philip, is anything wrong?' she asked, seeing the anxious, strained look on his otherwise cheerful features.

'I don't want to go, Annie. I don't want to. And they're making me...' Philip was incoherent, his words all spilling out together as he turned to her. He was nearly in tears, and he a big boy of nearly fourteen now. What ailed him?

'Calm down, love, and tell me, what is it? Here, let's walk a while.' Annie took him by the arm and steered him away from the house. She knew that if Molly was at home, Philip would be mortified to be seen crying in front of her. He adored Molly. Annie he regarded almost as a second mother. He had become very dependent on her when their parents had gone ahead to America, leaving Annie with Philip and Anthony in Cork. He had been only four years of age then, and had pined terribly for his mama, and it was to Annie he turned for solace rather than to Auntie Norah.

As they walked down the block away from the house, Philip told Annie that their parents would be off to Arizona within the month. They wanted him to accompany them.

Annie was taken aback. 'Are you sure, Philip? I understood they were not planning to go for some time yet. They haven't said a word about it to me. You must be mistaken.'

'No, it's true, Sis. Father got a letter a few days back from a friend of his out there who said that now is the time to come out. There's great opportunities for business, he says, now that there's so many mining for gold, silver and copper. He says...'

'Father, a gold miner, Philip. You can't mean it. He's far too old.' Annie stopped and stared disbelievingly at her brother. Old people didn't go prospecting for gold. Even Ellie's husband, Dan McAllister, had given up when he was quite young, to settle down and marry Ellie. It was preposterous.

'No, Annie, no. Father isn't reckoning on mining himself, but on starting a business.

On account of there are so many miners, businesses are springing up all over the place. Saloons, hotels, stores and suchlike.'

Annie nodded, understanding the logic of it but still shocked. Somehow, she had not really believed her parents would ever go west.

'But I want to stay here, Annie, don't you understand? I want to finish my apprentice-ship and become an upholsterer. Besides, I'm no kid. It's all right for the likes of Patrick and Lizzie – they're only babies and they don't know any better. But me... I want to get an education and work at my trade like Anthony and Tom. I'm nearly a man, after all,' he finished lamely.

Annie put her arm around him sympath-etically. 'Don't worry, Philip. Perhaps they are just worried about you and think you're too young to stay on here without them. But maybe if I talk to Father, you could stay with Tom and Anthony. Don't fret, it will come right. I'll go and talk to them straight away. We'll come up with something.'

True to her word, Annie wasted no time and went to speak with her parents that very evening. She found them both at home, Father poring over maps which covered the entire table. Mother seemed preoccupied but delighted to see her.

Philip was right. The Moores were indeed planning to take James O'Leary's advice and head off to Arizona with the children in tow by the middle of April at the latest.

'It will already be very warm by then,' explained Mother, 'and we want to be settled before it gets too hot.'

It seemed that James O'Leary – who lived in Phoenix – would have accommodation ready for them when they arrived and he would introduce Father to the local business community. *'We're looking for solid citizens to set up in business out here,'* he wrote. *'We need churches and schools and businesses out here if we're ever going to become a state.'*

'But what business, Father? How will you earn your living?' Annie was taken aback at her parents' apparently careless abandonment of everything they had worked for. What if they were to lose everything on this trip to nowhere? And to think her father had once called *her* foolhardy!

'Sit down, child. Sit down and we'll tell you all about it.' Annie did as she was bid and Father outlined his plan for a business he and Uncle Charlie planned to set up together. Such were the numbers of hard-rock copper miners flooding into Arizona Territory that there was an urgent need for all the equipment they required, from pickaxes to boots.

Father – who worked in a shirt factory and was now a floor manager – had been doing his research and was hoping to set up a shop selling all the garments that miners would need, like dungarees, shirts, breeches and jerkins. He had already found a manufacturer in New York and all he needed now was a small premises in Phoenix to use as a shop. Eventually, he and Charlie hoped to build up the business.

'And with your mother and Norah to help, we should have a modest business going in 'no time.' Father looked at her with such enthusiasm and determination that Annie just had to believe it was true.

A discussion followed on what Philip's future would be and, as Annie had suspected, her parents were anxious about him and were grateful for her advice. They reached a compromise. If it could be arranged that Philip would stay with Anthony and Tom, they would permit him to stay on in New York, at least until he could finish his apprenticeship. Then they would review the situation.

'But there could be a grand future for him out there, I'm sure of it,' said Father, set on having the last word.

And so it all happened very quickly after that. Her parents' grand adventure in life was only just beginning. Annie half-envied them. Her mother now seemed totally reconciled to the idea; indeed, she seemed excited at the thought that she would live in a house again rather than an apartment. Auntie Norah and Uncle Charlie did not plan to leave New York for a further six months, as Charlie would oversee the production of the stock from the New York end. Once that was up and running, they would join her parents in Arizona.

The whole family gathered at Grand Central Station on the evening of the Moores' departure on the long, long train journey across America. It was a fine April evening and, through her tears, Annie smiled to see her parents as excited as children. Heartbroken to part from them yet again, and with the little ones who she had barely had time to get to know, she was grateful to have Mike at her side, his arm protectively around her.

For all that Uncle Charlie and Auntie Norah were still with them, she knew it was only a matter of time now until they were off too. Philip looked bereft too, and even Anthony and Tom – though they would rather have died than show it – felt the breeze of loneliness blow about them that evening. It was a subdued and forlorn little group that waved the Western Pacific Express off on that occasion.

'Safe journey,' they cried, their voices getting lost in the hiss of steam. 'Write soon.'

6

MIKE BREAKS THE NEWS

The months flew by. Letters from Arizona were frequent and cheerful. The Moores' spirits were high, despite the heat of the summer months. They had become friendly with many other newcomers – some of them Irish like themselves – and seemed to have become caught up in a wave of pioneer enthusiasm for 'the Territory', as they all referred to Arizona.

They had a nice little house in the foothills of Camelback Mountain, one of the circle of mountains which surrounded the town of Phoenix. Here it was a little cooler than further down the valley. The children were as fit as fleas and Patrick had even started school. They described picnics in the desert and buggy rides up the Salt River to go swimming on Sunday afternoons. The landscape, they said, was magnificent, and the climate, despite the heat, dry and healthy.

Prospects for the fledgling business were good. Father had found a small premises and, more importantly, discovered that the potential for customers was more than promising. He was impatient for Charlie and Norah to join them and get down to work. His hard-earned savings were running low and could not be eked out for very much longer.

Meanwhile, Charlie and Norah were making progress with their plans for migration and would set off in September, accompanying the first batch of stock, which should be ready by then. Philip had stayed with them rather than with the boys for the past few months. He surprised everyone when the time for his aunt and uncle's departure approached by announcing that, now he had finished the first year of his apprenticeship, he would accompany them to Arizona and carry out his remaining studies there.

Annie was happy for him, as with the best will in the world she had not managed to see as much of Philip as she had intended. What with her teaching work, her meetings of the Women's Suffrage Association and her growing involvement in the refuge, she barely had any free time. When she did, she longed to spend it with Mike.

'Father and Mother are overjoyed that he's decided to go,' Annie told Mike as she read snippets of their most recent letter to him. 'Father feels sure he'll find work when his studies are finished, as there are a lot of people setting up home there.'

Mike nodded. He followed the Moores' adventures in Arizona with growing interest. He'd even profited from it in a small way when he got caught up in the garment workers' strike the previous May. There were over 34,000 garment workers in New York claiming to be grossly underpaid, and Mike's union, the Brotherhood of Tailors, had voted for strike action. As a result, he had been out of work for some weeks. Around the same time, Uncle Charlie had been looking for someone to give advice and practical help in designing the line of clothing he was planning to bring out to Arizona, and Mike had been grateful to oblige.

'It sounds as if they are all making good out there, you know. I don't think you need worry about them too much, Annie,' he said. 'Let us hope that if we go to war with Spain in Cuba, it won't have a bad effect on trade.'

'Do you really think it's likely to happen, then, Mike? The President keeps saying there will be no war.'

'Of course he doesn't want one, but it may yet happen,' Mike assured her. 'Now that he's appointed Teddy Roosevelt Assistant Secretary of the Navy, he may well find it inevitable. It's said that he is all for it. And you know he's right, Annie. Think of Ireland – a small country dominated by a larger one. That's what it's like for Cuba. They should be liberated from Spain. I would be all for a war myself.'

Annie looked at him in consternation. 'You're just like Carl,' she said. 'Why do men always want war?' As soon as she said the words she could have bitten her tongue off. She still hadn't got around to telling Mike about Carl.

'Carl?' queried Mike. Annie blushed scarlet and said, 'It's Gertrude's brother. He lives in Omaha ... well, no, he has gone to Arizona now. He ... he has gone there to join a bunch of men who are training for war, or something like that,' she finished, feeling confused and knowing she had not gone about things the right way. Now Mike would think there was something underhand going on.

Annie decided she had better tell him everything, now that she had started. So out came the whole story – how she had met Carl Lindgren when she had gone to stay with Gertrude in Omaha, how they had become friends, how she had been in a prairie fire with him and he had saved their lives, how he had declared his love for her and, most difficult of all to tell, how he still loved her and had written to her quite recently. When she reached the end of her story, Annie took a deep breath and looked up at her boyfriend.

Mike seemed a little taken aback. He stayed silent for a few moments and then said, 'And do you love him, Annie?'

'No, Mike, no. Of course I don't. I am fond of him, of course, but no,' she protested, 'I do not love him.'

No more was said on the matter, but somehow Annie felt that it had been left unresolved. If only she hadn't blurted out Carl's name in that way. If only she had told him at the start. Even though they didn't discuss it any more, from that time a shadow entered their relationship and it took some time to banish.

As summer deepened into autumn and Auntie Norah, Uncle Charlie and Philip departed for Arizona, Annie felt so lonely that she would have been lost if it weren't for Molly and Sophia and the refuge. Mike was working all hours, and when they did manage to spend some time together, he talked about nothing but the possibility of war. Molly said Tom did the same, but somehow that didn't make her feel any better.

In October the two girls hit on an ingenious plan for raising money to help Sophia and the Bright Angel Refuge. One evening they were returning from a meeting of the Women's Suffrage Association where Mrs Harriot Stanton Blatch had spoken at length about motherhood and had caused havoc by declaring that many American women were 'not fit to bring up their own children'.

'What a fuss about nothing,' Annie remarked to Molly on the way home. 'Think of the children at the refuge who are not even fortunate enough to have a mother. Why does she not speak about them?'

The two girls stood stock-still and looked at each other.

'That's it, Annie,' Molly declared excitedly.

'Don't you see? If Sophia had stood up to speak there this evening, she could have told a tale or two that would have put Mrs Stanton Blatch's talk in the shade. Wouldn't it?'

'Let's try and arrange for Sophia to speak to the association the next time,' suggested Annie, equally excited. 'And how about having a collection from the audience afterwards, in aid of the refuge? We could pass a box around. Some of the women there looked very well off, didn't they?'

Delighted with this inspiration, they sat down as soon as they reached home and composed a letter to the secretary of the Women's Suffrage Association, telling her about Sophia and the refuge and about their own involvement with it, and suggesting that their friend should speak at the very next meeting.

While it took a little while to persuade Sophia that this was a good idea, they eventually got her to agree to it when they mentioned that such a talk might yield an impressive amount of money for her cause.

Poor Sophia. On the one hand, she hated the idea of standing up to speak in front of a large crowd. On the other hand, she looked at the eager faces of her two friends and helpmates. They had done so much to help her already, coming several times a week to give the children classes – teaching them to read and write and do many a practical task. She could not very well refuse. Mike and Tom had been wonderful too, and besides organising an outing for the children to the Central Park Zoo, Mike had managed to get some funding for the refuge from his boss at work, Mr Bartholomew Gibson.

'Fine, I will do it,' she said finally.

It was a while before they even had a reply from the Association, but eventually it was agreed that Sophia should address the meeting in November. Mike also thought it a great idea and helped Sophia to compose her speech.

'You are accustomed to this kind of thing and poor Sophia is so timid,' Annie told him. 'With your help, she will be able to tell people how important this is.'

The evening finally arrived. Sophia's friend Jenny stayed at the refuge to look after the children, while Sophia, accompanied by her two friends, set off for the meeting. Indeed, not only did Annie and Molly attend, but Mike, Tom and all of Sophia's family were there to support her.

Annie was delighted to see the Rostov family again, associating them as she did with her very earliest days in America, when she had been frightened and timid and they had welcomed her into their family with kindness and warmth.

Alice Rodgers turned up too, pleased and proud to know Sophia, and sat with them all.

When Sophia was introduced and took her place on the platform the audience immediately fell silent. A slight figure in a well-worn cloak and unfashionable, sturdy boots, she didn't immediately strike that group of mostly well-off women as a likely champion of their cause. To most of them she looked like a poor young woman who needed looking after.

It wasn't long however, before this first impression was reversed and the initially sceptical expressions on their faces turned to interest as they became absorbed in the story Sophia had to tell them. Her dark eyes luminous, she spoke simply and directly about this project that had become so dear to her heart. She spoke of her work as a nurse and how it had led her to discover depths of poverty that she hadn't known existed. She described the helplessness of children whose parents had been carried away by disease or some other misfortune. She praised those who had helped her set up the refuge and who continued to support her. Then she spoke about the children – her little bright angels as she called them – who had been committed to her care and whom she could no more leave now than if they had been her own children. You could have heard a pin drop. Annie looked around her and saw tears in some of the women's eyes. She felt so proud of her friend and pleased that, at last she was receiving some well-deserved recognition for the work she was doing.

Sophia's talk received loud applause and this was reflected by the generous donations dropped into the box at the end of the evening. She was described by Mrs Lillie Deveraux Blake as 'a shining example of American womanhood' and as 'exactly the kind of modern woman America needs'. Poor Sophia looked very embarrassed and blushed to the roots of her hair at such unwanted attention.

They all returned to the refuge after the talk, elated by their success. Sophia was full of plans about what she could do for the children with the unexpected windfall.

'Well, they will surely enjoy a better Christmas than last year,' she concluded happily.

Christmas was indeed approaching fast, bringing with it a flood of letters from Arizona, Nebraska and even Ireland. Julia Donohue, Annie's old friend from Cork, wrote to tell of her betrothal to a Corkman. Annie was delighted to hear from her.

'Will you ever come back at all, Annie?' asked Julia. 'I still think about you and all the good times we had together. Remember me to your Auntie Norah and Uncle Charlie, and the boys too, of course. I am still teaching the piano but shall give it up when I am married and devote myself to other duties, I suppose.'

Somehow, Annie could not imagine Julia giving up her music, but then in Ireland, she remembered, most women *did* give up their work as soon as they married. It was considered a slur on the husband if he allowed his wife to work. It was as if he couldn't earn enough to keep a wife. Well, that wouldn't suit her at all, Annie thought, fuming inwardly at the thought. Then she recalled that as it was Mike she was expecting to marry, it would hardly be likely to happen to her anyway. At least, she hoped it would be Mike. Maybe he would not ask her. She had been having her doubts lately that he loved her as much as she'd thought. However, she dismissed these thoughts from her mind impatiently.

She was surprised – and not a little uncomfortable – to receive another letter from Carl. This time, she would tell Mike about it straight away, and show it to him. But after reading it, she realised that she couldn't risk showing it to him, as again, Carl had referred to his feelings for her.

I think about you and how you would love it here. I guess there is no hope that you would join me, else I would have heard it by now, he wrote.

Annie felt uneasy. It would be difficult to explain to Mike why Carl had expressed himself like this when she had not even written to him. She had given him no reason to believe that she returned his feelings.

Carl loved Arizona, he wrote, and although he felt sure that he would go to war in Cuba, he hoped he would be spared to return there and live his life in the desert. He seemed to have no doubt that there would be a war.

The family's letters from Arizona were full of their new life. Father wrote that the business was going very well and they were reordering goods all the time. The blue jeans and flannel shirts were going down especially well. Mother praised the climate.

It will be the first time we will spend Christmas in the sunshine, she wrote happily. *It seems so strange altogether, never having to wear a heavy cloak or a woollen shawl.*

Philip, too, wrote of his newly adopted home with enthusiasm, adding plaintively: *It would be just perfect if you and the boys were here too, Sis, but maybe some day you will come for a vacation and I will have so much to show you.*

Even Auntie Norah and Uncle Charlie could find nothing bad to say about their new home.

I miss you all and missed the city at first, wrote Norah, *but I must say this is a wonderful place, so different to anywhere I have been before. We are all well and healthy. There is such light and colour, even in winter, although you could hardly call it that, with it being so warm and all.*

Molly had invited Annie, Tom, Anthony and Mike to spend Christmas Day at her home in Brooklyn, and Annie was looking forward to it. Sophia would not be alone during the Christmas Season, as her family had decided to take turns helping her provide the children at Bright Angel Refuge with a real family Christmas.

They had all enjoyed another wonderful outing just before Christmas at the Carnegie Lyceum, when children from the Hebrew Technical School had entertained children from the Lower East Side at a large party. The girls were happy to see the children from the refuge have such a jolly time and the day had ended with the choirboys from St Patrick's Cathedral singing Christmas carols to the exhausted waifs. It was voted a great success by the sleepy crew of angels before they fell into their beds that night.

Even though Annie enjoyed Christmas Day with Molly's family, she sorely missed the absent members of her own family. She was surprised to feel so strongly about it, as she had greatly enjoyed the two consecutive Christmas seasons she had spent in Nebraska without them. She had a foreboding that something sinister was about to happen, and indeed on the day after Christmas, she knew it was no fancy notion she had taken, but very real.

Mike had been uncharacteristically quiet over Christmas, and when she finally questioned him about it, he replied that he had something on his mind.

'Annie, I know you will not be too happy to hear this, but I have decided to join up if we go to war with Spain,' he admitted finally.

Annie was stunned. She did not know why she should be, because Mike had spoken ceaselessly about the rights of the people in Cuba and how the American government should send a force to liberate them. Somehow, she had hoped and prayed that he would not take such an action. But what effect could she – a mere woman – have on him, after all, she thought angrily.

Unable to help herself, she burst into bitter tears. Mike did his best to comfort her, taking her in his arms, telling her he would be fine, that it might never come to pass, that it would be quickly over if it did, but nothing really worked and, though she soon dried her tears, Annie was deeply upset at the prospect.

She felt all the more bitter when she told Molly and discovered that Tom had no intention of joining up. While he felt sympathetic towards Cuba, he did not feel an obligation to join any voluntary movement to support them. Annie was happy for Molly, but she felt it was even more unfortunate that it should be her once-wild brother Tom who showed the kind of judgement and common sense that she had always attributed to Mike. She did not support this war with one inch of her being.

However, as the weeks went by, not wanting to dwell on the possibility of a parting from Mike, Annie persuaded herself that the business in Cuba would blow over and there would be no war.

It was all the more shocking when the news broke in the middle of February that an American battleship, the *Maine*, had been blown up in Cuba in Havana harbour, killing 258 American officers. There was uproar. Everyone said the Spanish were to blame. Mike was outraged and agreed passionately with this theory.

DESTRUCTION OF THE WARSHIP MAINE *WAS THE WORK OF AN ENEMY*, declared the *New York Journal*, offering a $50,000 reward *for the conviction of the criminals who sent 258 American sailors to their death*.

'War will surely be declared now,' Mike assured a horrified Annie.

He was right. Within the month, President McKinley asked Congress for a declaration of war. By 19 April, Congress had declared Cuba's independence and given the go-ahead to the President to send American troops to Cuba to fight the Spanish. *America*, wrote President McKinley, *must take up the cause of humanity*.

Annie was in despair. She knew now that nothing on this earth would stop her beloved Mike from joining up. What good now were her hopes and dreams of a future with him? What hope had she that he would ever come back alive?

7

TRAGEDY AT THE REFUGE

War was on everyone's lips. Although joining up was not compulsory, thousands upon thousands of young men like Mike and Carl felt strongly enough to want to jump into action instantly to support the liberation of Cuba. After war was finally officially declared on 21 April, President McKinley called for 125,000 volunteers to offer their services.

New York was festooned with flags and, if Annie had not been miserable over Mike's imminent departure, she could not have failed to become caught up in the patriotic fervour and enthusiasm for the war effort.

During his couple of days off at Easter, Mike had travelled to Washington to try and enlist in the army. As he was a good horseman from his boyhood days in Tipperary and a fair shot with a rifle, he felt he had a chance of being accepted in the First Regiment of Mounted Rifle Rangers. This was Teddy Roosevelt's own regiment – known as the Rough Riders – which was now recruiting men in the capital as well as in the west. The newspapers were full of stories of this colourful regiment because they were to be chosen mostly from among the cowboys and plainsmen of the far West. But there was also to be an Eastern contingent, and this was what Mike hoped to join. It was expected to be one of the finest fighting bodies in the country and would be at the head of the invading forces in the war.

As over 10,000 men had already been turned down for the Rough Riders Regiment, Annie felt that Mike's chances of being accepted were slim. However, she had not taken account of two things. One was Mike's determination to join this regiment at all costs, and the other was his political connections in Washington. So when he returned to New York on Easter Monday night, she knew the moment she saw him at Grand Central Station that her doubts had been without foundation and his mission had been successful.

'I'm in, Annie dearest, I'm in!' he cried, swinging her around like someone who had already won the war, single-handed.

Dumb with misery, Annie tried her level best to be cheerful and encouraging. They went directly to the tearooms, where Tom, Molly and Anthony awaited them. They all cheered when he announced his news.

'I might well join up myself,' declared Anthony excitedly, while even Tom looked as if his decision not to enlist had been a mistake. They all listened agog as Mike brought them up to date on the preparations for war. He himself, he said, would shortly be summoned to join his regiment in San Antonio,

Texas, where they would undergo intensive training before sailing for Cuba.

'I'll have to give in my notice at work tomorrow,' he said. 'They say my job will be there for me when I get back.'

As Annie looked from one to the other of her brothers, she saw how they listened to Mike with rapt attention. It would not greatly surprise her if Anthony *did* go out and enlist. He was eighteen, after all. She wondered what her parents would think of that. Tom, she knew, would not go to war. While he understood how Mike felt, he himself did not hold passionate opinions about Cuba and was amazed that America had declared war. Many people were against it and felt that a peaceful settlement could have been reached with Spain without taking such extreme action. She had to agree with him and hoped he would be able to bring some influence to bear in discouraging Anthony from joining up. She wondered again about Carl and was convinced that, by now, he too would have joined a regiment.

Later, as Mike walked Annie homewards, he broke the silence which had grown between them since they had left the tearooms. Pausing under a street lamp, he drew her towards him and looked down into her eyes, seeing the sadness and the fear. Cupping her face in his hands, he kissed her gently.

'I love you, dearest, and nothing changes that. I must do what I believe in or I could not live with myself. Do you understand that?'

'Yes,' said Annie quietly, 'I think I do.'

'I hope this war will be over within a few months. I will be back in no time, you'll see. Will you wait for me?' Now there was fear in Mike's eyes.

'Yes,' whispered Annie, trying hard to stop the tears from falling. But the tears were soon banished, as Mike enfolded her in his arms and kissed her ardently.

Annie was on tenterhooks over the next couple of weeks, waiting for Mike to announce the day of his departure. She threw herself wholeheartedly into her work in an effort to forget the fact that very soon they would have to part. She almost wished him gone, in the hope that the sooner he went, the sooner – if he was spared – he would return.

The dreaded day arrived. Togged out in his Rough Riders uniform, Mike cut a handsome figure among the men assembled at the train station. Annie could not help being proud of him. These days, the railway stations were often mobbed with departing troops, all heading off to the camps, from whence they would emerge transformed into fighting men with nothing on their minds but serving their country with honour.

A military band resplendent in uniform were tuning up to play when Annie and Molly arrived to see Mike off. Annie found it hard to keep smiling as they played 'The Girl I Left Behind Me' – it seemed everywhere you went these days they were playing that dratted tune.

'The girl I'm coming back to as soon as ever I can,' whispered Mike as they embraced for the last time. 'I'll write as soon as

I'm settled in the camp.' Annie nodded, unable to speak.

'Look after her for me, Molly,' called Mike as the train started to pull out and he finally had to step on and take his place among the cheering, waving men.

With all the strength she could muster, Annie tried to smile as she waved Mike goodbye. She did not want him to see her miserable, truly she did not.

'He'll be back, Annie, don't worry,' Molly said, placing a comforting arm around her friend's shoulders as she drew her away from the platform. 'Think how happy you'll be, the day you come here to welcome him home.'

Annie sat up in bed and rubbed her eyes. It was the second time she had heard someone cry out. It was the middle of the night and she and Molly had long retired to bed. Was she dreaming? No, there it was again. She jumped out of bed and looked out of the window into the street. Even from her position on the third floor, she could see someone jumping up and down, gesticulating. Yes, it appeared to be someone trying to get her attention. Could it be someone with news of Mike? Surely not, it was only a few days since his departure. Opening the window, she leaned out and saw that it was Peggy. Goodness, what was wrong with the girl? Had she been thrown out of the refuge or something?

'I'm coming, Peggy,' she called. At this, Molly awoke and hurried out of her room.

'What's the matter, Annie?'

Annie explained and the two girls hastily put on some clothes to cover their night things. They went quietly downstairs and out of the front door, hoping not to be seen by anyone.

'Miss Annie, Miss Molly, come quickly. Miss Sophia is sick and can't get out of the bed. Two of the bairns are sick too, and I don't know what to be doin'. Miss Jenny is not there, and ... and...' Peggy sounded frantic and it didn't take the girls long to see that she was totally in earnest. There was definitely a crisis at the refuge. Sophia needed them.

Telling Peggy to wait for them, they ran upstairs and dressed warmly, and within minutes were on their way. As they walked, Peggy filled them in on the details.

''Tis how Miss Sophia was lookin' after two of the little ones who were abed with a fever. They didn't appear to be gettin' better, no matter what we did. Miss Sophia was talkin' about bringin' them to the hospital if they hadn't improved by this mornin'. But then last night, she felt poorly herself and took to the bed. I woke up an hour ago to hear one of the sick bairns cryin' out, and when I went to fetch Miss Sophia, she was tossin' and turnin' and not a word of sense outta her. I didn't know what to do but to get help.' Distressed, she started to cry.

'You did right, Peggy, never fear, you did right,' Annie said, reassuring the girl and placing an arm around her thin shoulders. Even though it was May and the night was warm, Peggy was shivering.

Inwardly, Annie and Molly shivered also. It sounded serious. Dear God, prayed Annie, don't let it be typhus. There had been a number of cases reported in the newspapers again recently and talk of an epidemic to come. As usual, most cases reported were to be found in the poorer areas of town, like the Lower East Side.

Arriving at the refuge, they found chaos. All the children had awakened and were in confusion. The little ones were crying and calling for Sophia. While Molly set to restoring order and calm, Annie went into Sophia's room and lit the lamp. She was shocked at the sight of her friend, who was very flushed, her eyes staring unseeingly at the ceiling. She obviously had a very high fever. Annie did not waste a moment. She opened the window wide to let some fresh air in before fetching a sponge and a basin of cold water and starting to sponge her friend's forehead.

Then she went to check on the two sick children. One of them was awake and feverish, and crying fitfully, while the other one, a little boy called Sam – of whom she was immensely fond – appeared to be asleep but looked very ill. Peering closer, Annie was appalled to see the tell-tale red spots which suggested nothing so much as typhus. Oh no, she groaned inwardly.

Calling Molly to her side, she motioned her to examine the child for herself.

'We must fetch a doctor straight away,' whispered Molly. 'I'll go to the hospital.'

Luckily, Bellevue Hospital was not too far from the refuge, and Molly set off immediately, taking one of the older children to accompany her.

The next hour was one of the longest Annie had ever spent. If it proved to be typhus that had hit the refuge, she knew that quarantine would be considered very important. With Peggy's help, she moved all the children into the schoolroom and erected a makeshift screen around the sick children's cribs. As she worked, she wondered how many of the other children might already be sickening for this deadly disease.

With the help of God, it was some other malady. She knew there was no point in trying to contact Sophia's family or anyone else until medical help arrived.

She continued to sponge her friend down, hoping that if she became cooler she would come back to her senses. Was this really happening? She could not believe that Sophia – always cheerful and smiling, always on top of things – was reduced to this.

Just over an hour had passed when suddenly she heard the sound of bells followed by the clip-clop of horses' hooves. They came to a halt in the street outside. Thank God! The ambulance had arrived.

The children cowered in a corner as the basement premises suddenly seemed to fill with people. A doctor, accompanied by two nurses, immediately closeted himself with the patients while the ambulance men stood at the ready with pallets, to carry them out to the ambulance, should it be deemed necessary. By the time the doctor emerged and nodded to the ambulance men to move the patients, Annie and Molly hardly needed to be told what had befallen the occupants of the refuge.

'What is it, doctor?' Annie approached the doctor, who was looking very serious as he gave instructions to the nurse who accompanied him.

'Your friend is very ill,' he replied. 'We must get her to the hospital without delay. One of the children is also critical. It is typhus, I'm afraid, and you will all have to be examined at the hospital. There will be another ambulance along shortly, so get the children dressed and ready.'

There was no time for arguments or even further explanations. Annie and Molly did as they were bid, half-numb with shock. Sophia and the two children were whisked away in the ambulance within minutes and it wasn't long before she, Molly, Peggy and the remaining children were on their way to Bellevue Hospital in a second ambulance.

As they rode through the quiet streets, Annie remembered the time typhus had hit her neighbourhood in Monroe Street and the sense of dread that had accompanied it. Mother had warned them all not to go near the house where it had been found. As she saw the neighbours gather now in the grey gloom of early morning to watch the occupants of the refuge being borne away in ambulances, she recalled how she, some years earlier, had observed the same frightening scene.

She knew too, that within hours, the Disinfecting Corps would have arrived to fumigate the refuge, and it would then be closed down, and the occupants scattered. She wondered what would become of the children. What would happen to Sophia? Would she recover? She hardly dared to think about it.

She and Molly calmed the children as best they could. Hopefully they were not all infected with the disease. Even more unthinkable was the possibility that she and Molly might succumb to it.

As soon as the ambulance arrived at the great front doors of Bellevue Hospital, they were swept up the steps by waiting nurses and escorted swiftly to a nearby room. To the girls' horror, they noticed that everyone who attended them – nurses and doctors – wore masks on their faces.

They did not have long to wait before medical examinations began. Three more of the children were feared to be incubating the disease. The rest, including Peggy, were pronounced free of it. Neither Annie nor Molly were infected, according to the doctor.

'Not yet, anyway,' the doctor said. 'I will give you some medication, which you must start taking straight away. You must both take precautions for the next ten days and, if you develop any symptoms of illness whatsoever, you must come here to the hospital immediately. Nor should either of you attend work until I give you permission, as you would be a threat to the people you work with. However, because you have not been living in the refuge and have not been there for the past few days, I will release you, on condition that you keep in quarantine at home. A nurse will visit you each day to see how you are and to ensure that quarantine is observed.'

'What will happen to the children, doctor? Will they stay here in the hospital?' Annie asked tremulously.

'I am sorry to say we shall have to send them into quarantine on North Brother Island,' the doctor answered, looking around with pity at the bedraggled little group who now clustered around Peggy.

'And Peggy?' Molly ventured.

'She will have to go there too, I'm afraid, as she lived in the refuge. She will be a consolation to the little ones at least,' the doctor said.

Then Annie asked the question she had been trying to formulate for the past hour. 'What about Sophia? Will she recover?'

'She is critically ill,' the doctor replied gently. 'I don't know if she will recover. We'll know more in a day or two. Does she have a family?'

'Yes,' Annie replied. 'Perhaps I can tell

them. They might...'

'No, give me the address and the hospital will let them know. You must not visit anyone for the present, do you understand?' The doctor looked sternly at her.

It was also arranged that the hospital would inform Annie and Molly's schools that they would not be back at work for some days.

It was well into the morning before the two friends arrived home at their flat, exhausted and upset. They would have to write a note to Tom explaining what had happened. Annie also wrote a note to Alice Rodgers, who had been so impressed by Sophia's talk at the Suffrage Association meeting that she had offered to help out on occasional Sundays – her only day off. She did not want Alice to arrive at the refuge and find it closed up and abandoned.

Annie longed for the comfort of being able to confide in Mike. Why had he gone to war? She missed him so much. She must tell Tom not to write to her parents in Arizona with news of this – it would only worry them, and hopefully she and Molly would not come down with this terrible disease. Meanwhile, they had to be content to watch and wait.

Worse was to come. The following day, when the nurse arrived to inspect them, she told them that Sophia had taken a turn for the worse. Her parents were at her bedside and her chances of survival were now slim.

'But it cannot be true,' Annie protested, trying to stem the tears. 'Sophia has always been strong. Surely they can save her.'

'She is not as strong as you think,' the nurse responded. 'Her parents have been worried about her, as she has not been eating well since she went to live in the refuge. She felt she had to be careful, as she had so little money to get by. Her allowance was quite small.'

'May we go and see her?' Annie asked, her voice barely audible. She knew she was asking to be allowed say goodbye to her friend.

'It would be better not to,' the nurse said gently. 'It would be foolish to increase your risk of infection at this point. I will let you know how she is later.'

When the nurse left, Annie threw herself down on the settle and cried bitter tears. Sophia, her first and best friend in America, was to die. How could they have failed to prevent it? Perhaps if she had helped her more. She should have noticed that Sophia was not looking after herself. She had noticed that her friend had become very thin, but put it down to all the hard work she did to keep things going at the refuge. Maybe the refuge had become a trap for her friend. Maybe she had wished for an escape from it. Now, she realised, she would never know.

Molly comforted her as best she could. Although she too felt very sad, she had not known Sophia for as long as Annie had. Also, she had Tom to console her – not that she was allowed to see him until her quarantine was up, but she could write him notes. Poor Annie would be bereft, without Mike or her parents to turn to. She tried to keep her friend's spirits up but Annie was not to be distracted. She was sure now that Sophia would die of typhus.

Her premonitions were correct. Two days later, the nurse arrived at eight o'clock in the morning to break the news. Sophia Rostov had died in the night. Baby Sam had also died, an orphan child with scarcely a soul to mourn him. Even if he had survived, he would not have had much of a life to look forward to. Somehow the knowledge of this had made Annie weep all the more.

A week later, Annie and Molly were pronounced free of infection and were permitted to return to work. Sophia's funeral had taken place but they had not been permitted to attend. Annie had written to Sophia's parents, promising to visit as soon as she was free of quarantine. At least Annie had the comfort of knowing that Alice had attended the funeral in her place. The children from the refuge, along with Peggy, had been dispatched to North Brother Island. No one knew how long they would stay there. It was said that some people never returned from it.

Bright Angels Refuge – evacuated and fumigated – stood empty and forlorn, as if the happy laughter of the children it had sheltered for such a short time had never echoed through it. 'It's as if no one had ever lived there,' Annie said sadly to Molly.

Annie was grateful at that time for her two brothers, Tom and Anthony, who did their level best to console her and Molly. Alice Rodgers, too, shocked at the tragedy, visited frequently and did her best to comfort Annie – she had known both Annie and Sophia since they had started at the Phoenix Laundry four years previously. The pair had been friends since the day Annie had come to work there, she recalled.

Annie was heartbroken at the loss of her friend and the tragic circumstances of her death. She knew it was foolish, but she kept blaming herself for not having foreseen such a disaster.

All that kept her going during those dark days was her teaching work and the occasional letter from Mike, who – ignorant of what had happened at the refuge – wrote cheerful and colourful accounts of his life in the training camp in San Antonio. Although he wrote of events which meant nothing to her, Annie was grateful just to hear from him. That way she had the consolation of knowing that he was safe, at least for the time being.

8

NEWS FROM THE FRONT

Dearest Annie, wrote Mike, *since I last wrote to you we have been moved to Tampa in Florida, from where we shall very shortly sail for Cuba. The Navy has set sail ahead of us and we are now impatient to be off. We are ready to honour the flag and take up arms, and every man among us is determined to show what stuff we are made of. It has been a hard time here in Florida, what with the heat and the mosquitoes. Many have been ill with dysentery, but never fear, I am strong and healthy.*

You would be surprised at how well we troopers from the city mix with the wild cowboys of the West. They call us the 'tenderfeet', or sometimes, when they really want to make fun of us, it's the 'Fifth Avenue Boys'. They have no trouble riding the Texan mustangs we'll be using in battle and they are a mean shot with the rifle. We had a lot to learn from them.

Lieutenant Colonel Wood heads up the regiment, but it is Colonel Roosevelt who is the real leader. He's the one person in the camp whom every single man admires and obeys without question. Although of a very well-got family and from a high position in government, he willingly gave it all up to fight for this cause. They say he spent some years out west living the life of a rough rider himself and that is why he recruited so many men from there. And wild they are. One of them is Captain Buckey O'Neill – he leads the Arizona regiment, who are mostly cowboys. He is mayor of Prescott, Arizona, and they say he is the bravest man in the whole West. I'd guess your parents have already heard tell of him out there.

I was glad to get your letters, even though they can take a long time to come, as they have to go through government offices first and are then sent on with mail from everywhere else. You don't say much. I hope all goes well with your work and that the Bright Angels are thriving. Sophia must be happy that you have more time to help out as I am not there to distract you.

At this, Annie put the letter down. She had not had the heart to tell Mike of the terrible tragedy that had befallen Sophia and the refuge. She still felt this was the right thing to do. He had a difficult task to confront shortly and he would have been devastated to hear what had happened since he left. But in not telling him, she had found it difficult to write with enthusiasm about anything else. Heavy of heart though she was, she determined at once to write to him in more cheerful tones. Soon enough he would be on the battlefield and then she would have to depend on the newspapers for news of his doings. Only a day later she received a letter from Carl, also postmarked Tampa, Florida. He wrote that he too was a member of the Rough Riders Regiment and serving under the famous Captain Buckey O'Neill. What an amazing coincidence! Surely by now he and Mike had met. What would they think of each other? But of course Carl knew little of Mike, and Mike knew even less about Carl. They could be friends already and not know of her connection with each of them. They were undoubtedly going to be comrades in arms.

In some strange way, the thought cheered Annie up. She knew in her heart that if they were meant to meet, they would, and she for one was sure they would like each other. Sure didn't they have one thing in common in loving her? Smiling for the first time in weeks at her own boldness, Annie sat down to write to her beloved. He would need all the support he could get in the coming weeks.

She wrote: *I've had another letter from Gertrude's brother, Carl Lindgren, and you will be very surprised to hear that it came from Tampa. He writes that he serves under the very Captain Buckey O'Neill you were telling me about. I have not written to him, so he knows nothing at all about you going to war. You remember I told you about him going to Arizona with the hope of joining up? So it seems that you might get to make his acquaintance – I should be very glad if you did, as his family were very kind to me when I lived in Nebraska. I think you would find him among some of those wild Western cowboys you were writing about. As for me, I prefer my Fifth Avenue man any day. I do not know if he can be called a tenderfoot but I sure know he is tender of heart.*

Annie knew she would wait for some time for a reply, if indeed she received one before he sailed. She was all the happier that she had managed to write to Mike in a more positive manner. She knew he would treasure her loving words of reassurance. Annie felt that refusing to buckle under the shadow of the days and weeks ahead could only draw them closer and give her courage, whatever lay in store for them.

However, when she read in the newspaper a week later that the Rough Riders had departed aboard the warship *Yucatan* for active service in Cuba, she thought her heart would stop. There was nothing she could do now but pray.

As the end of the school year approached, both Annie and Molly started to make plans for the long summer ahead. Both planned to look for work during the school vacation. Annie toyed with the idea of calling into Miss Gilroy at A. & T. Stewart's to see if she could get some summer work at the store. Molly had an even more important reason to earn some extra money as she and Tom planned to marry shortly.

The wedding, which had been planned for the end of July, had been postponed, as Mike had promised to be Tom's best man.

The young couple felt that it would be a vote of confidence in his safe return if they postponed their marriage until the war was over. They had now set a date for December, when they hoped he would be back in New York, safe and sound. Molly had invited Annie to be her bridesmaid and the two young women were full of plans for the big occasion.

'You'd better pay close attention to how it's done, Annie,' teased Molly one evening, 'as it's likely you'll be heading for the church yourself before too long.'

Annie laughed and changed the subject. How could she tell her friend, so happily absorbed in her wedding plans, that she could not dare to indulge such daydreams with Mike's fate hanging in the balance?

Who could tell when the war would be over? It could go on for a couple of years, for all any of them knew. However, entering into Molly's plans gave her a sense of purpose and was one way of convincing herself that Mike would return unharmed.

While Annie had enjoyed her six months of teaching at St Margaret's, she had not found it as satisfying as her time working in the small, one-roomed prairie school in Kimball. There she had found herself more able to help the children under her care. Because it was a small school, she had been able to get to know each child, as indeed she had come to know their families. At St Margaret's, she worked with large groups of children and could be moved from one class to the other at short notice. However, she hoped that when she returned to work in September, she would get to stay with one group for at least a term.

Every day Annie scanned the newspapers for news of the war. The *Herald*, the *Journal*, the *Post*, the *World* and *Harpers' Weekly*, were all sending back detailed reports of the war in Cuba. In the last days of June, it became known that eight Rough Riders had been killed in the battle of Las Guasimas. Sick with worry, Annie went straight to the offices of the *New York Herald* after work to see the latest newsflashes and try to secure a list of the casualties.

Knowing that a friend of Mike's, Ed Reilly, was a journalist with the paper, Annie asked for him at the front office. She hoped that he would be able to find out something for her. She had only met him once, but she was planning to explain who she was.

Ed needed no reminder of who Annie was and greeted her warmly, steering her away from the crowds in the front office and down a corridor into the newsroom. Annie explained why she had come and he was immediately sympathetic.

'The names have not been released yet,' he told her. 'I'm sure there's no need to worry but I'll speak to the news editor and see if he can tell us something.'

Sitting her down at a spare desk, he walked the length of the newsroom to where an older, harassed-looking man seemed to be giving orders to everyone at once. Annie looked around her. She had never been in a newspaper office before and was amazed at the scene of hectic activity. There were desks everywhere in the vast room, with a type-writer standing on each of them. The journalists were either typing on the machines so fast she could hardly see their fingers moving or talking animatedly to colleagues, their shirtsleeves rolled up and cigarettes hanging out of the corners of their mouths. It was very noisy in the room, as the din of machinery was occasionally punctuated by the shrill ringing of a telephone.

Ed was back within minutes. 'Annie, it's good news. We are not free to release the list of those killed yet, but I can assure you that Mike is not on it. Nor is the Carl Lindgren you mentioned.'

Annie felt a huge surge of relief. 'Thank God,' she said.

'Now, why don't I show you around the place since you're here,' Ed offered.

'I'd like that,' Annie replied, smiling for the first time. 'Is it always so busy?'

'Well, I reckon it is but it's especially busy just now with the war reports coming in all the time. We're looking for extra hands at the moment. Hey, I don't suppose you can take copy, can you?'

'Well, I can use a typewriter,' Annie answered hesitantly, wondering what 'take copy' meant.

'That's capital,' said Ed. 'How would you like to come and work for us for a while? You just said you're a teacher, and I guess you'll shortly be on vacation.'

'Yes, that's true. I'd sure like to give it a try,' said Annie, warming to the idea by the minute. She had managed to keep up her typing skills by practising on the machine at St Margaret's, where she had helped Miss Donnelly by typing the pupils' end-of-year reports.

'Now, we can only pay you $15 a week and you might have to keep late hours occasionally. When could you start?'

The visit to the *Herald* office took Annie's breath away. She had gone there with the sole intention of finding out if Mike was safe, and not only had she found out he was, but she had emerged with a summer job. How she longed to tell Molly she was going to work for a newspaper! How proud Mike would be! But the best thing about it was that she would be right on the spot to hear the latest news bulletins from the war. She was sure Ed would keep her informed. In some small way, the idea of working there made her feel closer to Mike.

She could hardly wait until term ended and she was free to start. There was another week to go and she used it well, staying back at the school most afternoons to practise on the typewriter. She guessed she might also have to use the telephone – a complicated device, she thought, every time she saw one – but she was sure she would soon become accustomed to it. Then there were the new linotype machines Ed had proudly shown her. These printed out the news reports faster than any machine had ever done before, Ed explained. There was so much to learn.

Within a week, Annie was installed at the

New York Herald office. Far from being able to sit around reading news reports from Cuba, she immediately became swallowed up in the great hub of activity that went into producing a daily newspaper. She hadn't a moment to worry about Mike, Carl or the war. If she wasn't typing out the reports sent in by reporters around the city, she was making coffee or running errands for the busy editors. It sometimes reminded her of her brief spell as a runner in the Fulton Fish Market a few years previously.

There was a particular air of excitement when she entered Herald Square on her way to work on 2 July. She saw a crowd gathered outside the *Herald* office, gazing intently up at the illuminated message board.

'LATEST FROM CUBA – OVER 1,000 AMERICAN CASUALTIES IN BATTLE AT SAN JUAN HEIGHTS,' it read.

Annie stood rooted to the spot. This was the worst news yet. Sick with fear, she ran into the office, hoping that Ed would be there and could find out what she most feared to ask. Rather than the gloom she had expected, she found there was uproar in the newsroom. Reporters were in a wild state of excitement. The number of dead or injured, it seemed, represented some sort of victory. One journalist jumped over a desk and threw his hat in the air, shouting, 'We've won! We've won the war!'

There was no sign of Ed Reilly, the one person whom Annie knew well enough to approach. Then she recalled he was working on the late shift that week. Timidly, but resolutely, she approached the news editor's desk. As usual, he had a group of reporters standing attentively around him awaiting instructions.

'Yes, what is it? Ain't you got enough work to do, young lady?' he barked at her irascibly, not welcoming the interruption.

'Excuse me, sir, but could you let me see the list of casualties from Cuba? You see, my ... well, that is ... someone I know is out there with the troops and I need to know if he is all right.'

There was a moment of shocked silence at her temerity before a smile began to spread across the editor's face. A couple of the reporters started whistling 'The Girl I Left Behind Me'.

'Ah, so you have a sweetheart in the troops, is that it?' He looked around. 'Now whaddya think of that, boys? This young lady is fretting over her sweetheart. Ain't that cute?'

Annie could feel the tears coming. She knew that if she let herself cry, she would never live it down. Feeling her cheeks grow as red as fire, she made to turn away, regretting her naivety in asking him outright. She should have waited until Ed's shift started. He could have got the information for her.

'Okay, okay now, young lady. Hang on there. You gotta right to know. Ain't that true, boys? She's gotta right to know. As soon as I find out, you'll find out. Okay? We have a deal?'

Seeing that he was actually trying to be kind, Annie nodded dumbly and returned to the desk outside in the lobby where she and another girl sat squashed into a corner, sharing a desk supplied with two type-writers.

There then followed the longest day Annie could remember. There was a lot of talk about the battle which had taken place in Cuba the day before. The telegraphs were coming in all morning with fresh details about it. She knew she would have to wait until Ed came in to find out. She daren't approach the editor again. He had not even asked her the names she wanted to check, and he seemed to have forgotten all about it anyway.

Finally, as she was about to leave, Ed came in to work the evening shift. 'Ed, please, can you help me?' Annie called after him as he rushed by hurriedly.

Again, Ed was kindness itself. Annie waited outside in the corridor and it seemed an age until he returned. He looked sombre, however, as he strode towards her.

Oh no – he has bad news, it can't be … thought Annie, feeling as if her legs might go from under her.

But his first words were, 'Mike's not on the list of those killed, Annie, although he could well be injured.' He paused. Evidently there was something else.

'Ed?' Annie prompted, puzzled.

'Your other friend, isn't he called Carl Lindgren?' asked Ed, looking at her and glancing down at the piece of paper on which he had copied down Carl's name. 'I am afraid there's bad news about him, Annie. He was on the list. I am sorry. He was killed in battle.'

Annie was struck dumb. Carl dead? She could not believe it. He who could escape from a fierce prairie fire unscathed – dead? She had always been sure that if either of them died, it would be Mike. She had not considered for a moment that it would be Carl.

Thanking Ed abruptly, she left the office and made her way home in a state of numb shock. Unbidden pictures of the Carl she had known in Nebraska plagued her – the time they had danced together at Gertrude's wedding, the trip they had taken on horseback out on the prairie and the interesting tales he had told her about Nebraskan wildlife, but most of all how he had saved her life the day of the prairie fire. And now he was lying, dead, out in Cuba.

Annie was glad of Molly's company that night. She had never told her friend much about Carl, or what had passed between them. That evening, however, she confided in her, recalling for her the time Carl had saved her life and how his feelings for her had blossomed from friendship to love – a love she could not return, as even then she knew she loved Mike.

'Oh Molly, I feel so badly. I never even replied to his letters. I should at least have done that,' she sobbed while Molly comforted her as best she could.

'Shush, Annie, it would have been worse to have led him on. And you would have had to tell him about Mike eventually.'

'I can't bear to think how his family will suffer. I must write to them straight away. I must write to Aunt Marthe, too – she will be so sad. She was very fond of him.'

Eventually Annie calmed down and was comforted once again by the thought that Mike had escaped death. But had he been injured? How would she find out? Hopefully, if the war was now nearly over, she would hear from him herself. That night, however, her dreams were fraught with scenes of battle, the sound of guns and the sight of bloodshed. She kept dreaming that it was Mike who had been killed and woke up, choking with terror.

In the days that followed, Annie learned that, while the Battle of San Juan had indeed won the war for America, there had been heavy losses. Six and a half thousand men had fought in the battle – the Rough Riders Regiment included. Out of 1,300 casualties, 205 were killed and 1,180 wounded. Later she was to hear that sixteen Rough Riders had been killed. Carl was one of the unlucky ones.

The rumour had got around the newspaper office that Annie had received bad news about the war, so at least there was no more teasing, and she was grateful for that. She gathered that, despite the fact that the Americans had won a moral victory over the Spaniards, the battle wasn't quite over yet and it would be some time before the troops could disengage. The biggest threat now was illness – apparently dysentery and malaria were rife among the troops already, while there was a serious threat of yellow fever.

The *Herald* office continued to be busy, with endless reports of the diplomatic tactics necessary to bring the war to a close as well as tales of illness and occasional deaths among the sick and wounded troops.

Annie was grateful to be able to continue working at the newspaper, as she found the only way to get through that terrible summer was to be fully occupied. First Sophia's death, then Carl's, and now the long wait to hear if Mike was safe and healthy. Much as she appreciated having Molly around, she had never missed her family as much as she did now. She found letters inadequate to express how sad and bereft she felt.

Towards the middle of July, she received a heartbroken letter from Gertrude:

We can hardly believe Carl is gone from us for good. My parents were very much against him going to Arizona last year, as they knew he would join up if war was declared, but they could do nothing to stop him. The worst is that he has been buried in a mass grave near the battlefield and all they could send us was his watch and his stripes. A letter from the Colonel said that he was a hero and had died 'a truly gallant death and distinguished himself in the line of duty'. Although we are proud to hear this, we wish that his body could have been brought home and buried here, where he belonged. Papa will never recover, as he depended greatly on Carl and there is no one now to take over the farm.

A couple of weeks later, solace arrived at last in the form of a letter from Mike. He had returned to Florida along with the other wounded men, where he would be billeted until further notice:

I have been wounded in the leg and am in hospital here. I have also had malaria but am quite recovered. But believe me, dearest, these trials are nothing to what has been suffered by some. I was fortunate to have escaped with my life. Yes, my love, I got to know your Carl and I know that by now you will have heard of his death in the Battle of San Juan. He died very courageously in the front line of battle, in a rush up Kettle Hill. I wasn't far behind him, but when I got to him he was already dead. I was able to salvage his watch, which the Colonel sent to his family.

I had got to like him very much and see why you liked him so. When I explained who I was and what you and I were to each other, he was very gracious and said I was a lucky man and he'd shoot me without hesitation if I were ever to let you down. I reckon he'd have done it, too. I thanked him for saving your life in the prairie fire and he seemed happy to know that you had told me about it. On the same day, and indeed before the battle had started, the officer of his troop – one of the best officers in the entire regiment – Captain Buckey O'Neill, was felled by a sniper's bullet. That was another great loss – a man who was not only Carl's hero, but a man I had also come to admire greatly.

My dearest love, I have missed you more than I can say. I have kept your last letter safely in a pocket close to my heart along with your picture all these months and they have afforded me much comfort. I hope to be back to New York in a month or so, when I shall want to ask you something very particular and will hope for a very particular answer. I think – I hope – that we have much to plan and discuss.

Your loving Mike

This time Annie's tears were tears of joy. The long wait was nearly over.

9

THE WAR IS OVER

The scene at Grand Central Station was one of chaos. Returning soldiers and their relatives mobbed the platforms and the joyful cries of welcome mingled with shouted warnings from porters trying to transport the wounded safely on stretchers through the crowds.

Annie could not see Mike anywhere. 'Surely he couldn't be on a stretcher, could he?' she asked Molly and Tom, who were also trying to spot him. Suddenly, Anthony – who was positioned further down the platform, towards the end of the train – let out a yell of delight and ran forward, arms outstretched. Annie was fast on his heels to welcome her beloved: a thinner, paler, but smiling Mike, who was making his way towards them with the aid of a stick.

'Mike, at last,' were the only words she could manage before she was in his arms and felt his lips on hers. After a long moment, they drew apart to find Molly, Tom and Anthony all grinning broadly and waiting to say their words of welcome. The war was over at last.

Annie thought that she could not easily have surpassed the happiness she felt at that moment. But she was proved wrong later that evening, when after a wonderful welcome-home meal at Tom and Mike's apartment, she and Mike were alone at last.

Taking her hand in both of his and looking at her very seriously, Mike said, 'Annie, I had a lot of time to think while I was away – think about you and what you mean to me. I came to realise that I love you even more than I had thought possible. I know now I want to spend the rest of my life with you and never be parted from you again. I had thought it would be proper to wait and speak to your father when the time was right, but now I know the time *is* right, your father is far away and I cannot wait any longer. Will you marry me, Annie, my love?'

Though she had long known this moment was inevitable, Annie was moved by the passion in Mike's voice and her own response was equally heartfelt.

'Oh, Mike, I will, of course I will,' she replied, throwing her arms around him and burying her face in his neck. 'I cannot tell you how I feared for your life, and how I thank God you were spared to come back to me.'

With that, Mike drew out a small box and opened it. Inside lay a little gold ring with three precious stones glittering in a delicate twisted cluster. Ceremoniously, he placed it on the third finger of her left hand. Annie looked at it in wonder.

'My betrothed,' Mike whispered, drawing her to him.

Some time later they called in the other three, who had withdrawn to the kitchen on the pretext of washing dishes. Much was the rejoicing that followed the couple's happy announcement, with Anthony joking that he had better get cracking or he'd be left an old bachelor.

Annie had long left the summer job at the *Herald* newspaper and was back working at St Margaret's while Mike was still on sick leave and under doctor's orders not to return to work until his leg – which had been severely wounded by a bullet – was completely healed. Fortunately for a young man who was planning to wed, the army would pay him a disability allowance until he was well enough to return to work. But these were happy days, and each afternoon Annie went straight to see him before doing anything else. They had so much to catch up on and so much to plan.

With the agreement of Tom and Molly, a double wedding in December was decided upon. It took very little rearranging, except that now, of course, Mike could not be Tom's best man, nor Annie Molly's maid of honour. That little problem was soon solved by Tom inviting his brother Anthony to do the honours, while Mike was to ask his old political pal Billy Farrelly.

Molly would now ask her cousin Mary Anne to be her maid of honour. Annie, who keenly felt the loss of Sophia, had yet to think of someone to ask. If only Ellie or Gertrude did not live so very far away.

'Annie, I've been thinking about our future and making plans, but there is something I have been thinking about for a long time which I would like to put to you,' Mike said one afternoon, shortly after his return.

'You haven't another war up your sleeve, I hope,' joked Annie. 'I don't think I could bear another one so soon.'

'No, although I did think about it while I was in Cuba,' replied Mike. He paused for a moment, then continued. 'I met quite a number of people from Arizona in the camp and I was impressed by them,' Mike began. 'I told you about Captain Buckey O'Neill, the officer from our regiment who was shot. He was originally from Washington but went out to Arizona as a young man because he heard there were lots of opportunities there. He made a good life for himself there and became a newspaperman, working first in Phoenix, then Tombstone, and finally Prescott, where he became a politician. Eventually, before he enlisted for the war, he became mayor there. But besides doing all that, he also explored the Grand Canyon, and got to know it so well that he became a guide. He gave us great descriptions of the beauty of the landscape and made it sound like the best place on earth to live. He said he would never return east.'

Annie was listening attentively but said nothing. Mike went on. 'Then I got to thinking about what a success your family has made out of the business they set up and how they also love the climate and the life there. Before I went off to war, when I was helping your Uncle Charlie out with the stock he was bringing out there he told me that if I ever wanted to join them and take over the manufacturing side of it, I would be welcome. Then there's politics. Arizona is working hard at getting into the Union and becoming a state, and it would be exciting to get involved in politics there now. I must say, I have thought about all this quite a lot, but the war came and I had no chance to discuss it with you until I returned. What do you think about it all?'

Annie's smile had grown wider as he spoke, and her eyes were shining. 'I didn't think you would ever consider leaving New York, Mike Tierney,' she said. 'Naturally, I would love to join my family. But going out there with you to start a new life would be a dream come true! Maybe it will even be the next state to give women the vote. And I could teach, because they are not so strict about the rule barring married women from teaching out in the Territories, are they?'

'Even if they were, my love, you would find plenty to do in that kind of society. You could maybe join me in the business, or we could even start up a business of our own eventually. There are so many possibilities.' He smiled down at her. 'So you will agree to it, then?'

'Let's write to the family straight away,' cried Annie impulsively.

'No, we should discuss this fully first. We have so much to decide,' Mike said. 'Besides, I must first of all write to your father and ask for your hand in marriage. I have done everything the wrong way around. Do you think he will refuse me?' Mike asked, his eyes twinkling.

'He wouldn't dare,' replied Annie, knowing full well that her father would not only be pleased with her choice of husband, but not in the least surprised.

Many happy hours were spent by the young couple over the following days discussing and mapping out their future. When should they go? Should they wait a year or two or go right away? Would the family still want Mike to join them in the business?

'Sure, they couldn't get a better tailor!'

Annie stated emphatically.

Gradually a plan emerged and they set it all out for discussion with Molly and Tom, who were flabbergasted initially at their decision, but soon became infected with their enthusiasm and began to think it made good sense.

'How I will miss you, Annie. Perhaps some day we can join you,' Molly said wistfully.

However, Tom's ambitions were very definitely centred on New York, where he hoped to be nominated as a candidate for the New York City Council in the near future. Anthony also planned to stay on in New York. Nothing, he said, would persuade him to live in the desert.

'I will miss you too, Moll, and you, Tom,' said Annie. 'We both will, but you know it's becoming cheaper to travel all the time. We will see plenty of each other, you'll see.'

They had written to Annie's parents – as well as to Mike's family in Ireland – of their plans. The couple now planned that as soon as they were wed in December, Annie would move in with Mike and they would depart for Arizona by the beginning of the new year. Mike planned to give in his notice shortly, while Annie would be able to stay on at St Margaret's until the end of term. Tom and Molly had already found an apartment to live in.

Needless to say, an ecstatic letter soon arrived from Arizona. The Moores could not have been more pleased at the news.

We cannot say which pleases us more, wrote Mother, *that you will marry Mike or that you are coming out here to join us.*

They repeated with great enthusiasm their offer to Mike to join the business and said they would have rooms rented for the newly married couple to live in on their arrival.

Housing is not as expensive here as in New York and we are sure that, like us, you will be able to buy your own home before too long, Mother wrote.

Auntie Norah and Uncle Charlie were to travel to New York for the great occasion, she added. Charlie had to oversee the ordering of more stock for the business in Phoenix and would also take Father's place in giving Annie away, while Auntie Norah would be happy to act as her matron of honour if required. Annie couldn't have been happier.

Mike too had good news when his brother Sean, who was a priest, wrote offering to come to New York and perform the marriage ceremony for the two couples.

The only shadow to darken their happiness at that time was the tragedy of Sophia's death and the fate of the Bright Angel Refuge. Annie had been to see the Rostovs on a couple of occasions, only to return in tears at the extent of their heartbreak over the loss of their lovely daughter.

Annie, who had just begun to come to terms with the tragedy, now had to relive it as she saw Mike's shocked reaction to it. Together they resolved to try and find out what had become of Peggy and the children, of whom nothing had been heard since they had been placed in isolation on North Brother Island.

Annie and Molly had already been to Bellevue Hospital to ask if anything was known about their whereabouts, but they had not been able to get any information about them.

'They would not be returned here, in any case,' one of the nurses explained. 'If the children recovered, they would have to be sent to an orphanage, but I do not know what would have become of the older girl you mention.'

Annie felt particularly responsible for Peggy, who had been so happy at the refuge – happy, she guessed, for the first time in her life. She could have returned to her family, of course, but they had thrown her out long ago. The thought that she was out there begging on the streets again as winter approached did not bear thinking about.

It was a welcome surprise, therefore, when she arrived home one evening to find Peggy sitting on the steps of the house, looking a bit skinnier than usual, but not too dishevelled.

'Oh Miss Annie, Miss Annie, I thought as how you'd left this place and gone somewhere else,' she cried, her face lighting up with relief.

'Peggy, thank God you're all right then. How about the children? What happened? Where have you been all this time?' Annie put her arms around Peggy and hugged her with delight.

Smiling all over her face with pleasure at this welcome, Peggy followed Annie upstairs to the flat, where she received a similar welcome from Molly. She soon filled them in on all the details. All the children had survived, she said, and had been taken back to New York eventually and placed in different orphanages around the city.

'But it was a terrible place altogether,' she told them, shuddering at the memory. 'All the people who had typhus was in the same place and, no matter if you were dyin', you were put in with the ones who was gettin' better. And the ones who was gettin' better had to help with the sick ones. And there was more cryin' from the bairns and moanin' from the sick ones that you couldn't hear yourself think.'

Annie and Molly smiled at one another.

'But when did you get out of there, Peggy?' Molly asked.

'A couple of months back,' replied Peggy. 'They had to let my mother know where I was and they made her take me back. She wasn't best pleased, but she says I must get out now and fend for meself or else bring in some money.' She looked hopefully at the two girls, who knew they would now have to try and find something for Peggy to do.

At least Peggy still had a roof over her head, but it sounded as if this might not last too long if she didn't get a job.

It was Mike who suggested that they bring it up at the next women's suffrage meeting they attended. After all, there were a lot of women there who were quite well off, and they might know of a place going as a servant somewhere. Not that Annie felt that she could really recommend Peggy as a general servant, having worked with her at the Van der Leutens'. But if they could find her work looking after children, she might be very good. After all, Sophia had found her to be a great help, and nursery maids were much in demand in New York.

'Leave it with me,' the president of the association, Mrs Lillie Deveraux Blake, said when the girls confided in her before the meeting. It was her custom to make announcements about a variety of things when the main business of the evening had been dealt with.

It was a week later when Annie and Molly had a note from Mrs Deveraux Blake suggesting that they bring Peggy along to meet one of her ladies, who was desperately searching for a nursemaid for her little boy. She had a full complement of other staff and wanted someone purely to devote themselves to the child during the day. It would be a live-in position.

Peggy was thrilled when she heard and could not thank the girls enough. 'I hope I won't let yez down, now,' she said anxiously.

Peggy did not let them down. Accompanied by Annie, she went along to be interviewed. By a piece of good fortune, the woman of the house was of Irish background and was more accepting of Peggy than many New York matrons might have been. This in turn gave Peggy confidence, and she agreed to start right away.

Annie and Molly were jubilant. This would be a fresh start for Peggy. Not only did they feel she deserved a little good fortune at last but they felt sure she would make a success of it. Sophia, they knew, would have been proud of her.

As the weeks passed, the two young women became very busy, organising the details of their joint wedding, which was set for 10 December at St Brigid's Church on nearby Tompkin's Square. The parish priest, Father McSweeney, had been more than helpful and readily accepted the prospect of Mike's brother, Father Sean, performing the ceremony.

The wedding breakfast would be held at

the Excelsior Hotel, where Tom worked, and where they had received a favourable rate. To it they had invited Molly's whole family, some of Mike and Tom's friends and Sophia's family, as well as Annie's old friend Alice Rodgers. Then, of course, there would also be Uncle Charlie and Auntie Norah.

Molly and Tom were planning a wedding trip to Washington, while Annie and Mike were content to forgo one, as within weeks they would be making the long journey to Arizona. But the two couples looked forward to spending Christmas together in New York, along with Anthony, who had now moved into a new flat with some friends at work.

Annie had written to Ellie and Dan as well as Gertrude and Aunt Marthe of her betrothal to Mike, inviting them all to the wedding. She received delighted replies on all sides but no assurances that her friends could attend. Nobody from Gertrude's family could travel at that time. So her joy knew no bounds when one morning she opened a letter written in Ellie's familiar hand announcing that she and Dan and the children would travel to New York for the wedding. As it would be December, there would be little to do on the farm and Ellie's brother-in-law John and his boys would keep an eye on things for a few weeks.

To her added delight, they would bring Ellie's niece Laura with them to take the opportunity to have a look at the millinery business in New York and see if perhaps she could make a go of it in the big city herself. Annie was delighted that she would see Laura once again. They had been friendly while Annie had lived in Nebraska and had written to each other a few times since. Laura – who was well on the way to becoming a talented milliner – had always wanted to come to New York and now she was getting the perfect opportunity.

We plan to stay on over Christmas and give ourselves a real holiday, wrote Ellie. *Dan has a sister living in New York and she has invited us to stay many times. Besides, she is dying to meet our children, as she hasn't laid eyes on either of them yet.*

'Oh Molly, I am so happy!' Annie exclaimed. 'Now you and Mike and Tom will get to meet Ellie and Dan. I know you will love them.'

Although it would have been perfect if her parents and Philip had also been able to come, Annie was well contented now that at least Charlie and Norah would be there to represent her parents on the most important day of her life. And Mike, who knew her thoughts were much with her two lost friends and absent family during this time, was happy for her.

10

THE BIGGEST ADVENTURE OF ALL

Annie awoke early on the morning of her wedding. Knowing it would still be dark outside, she lay on in bed, looking around the room she had occupied for the past two years. The closets were empty, except for her white satin wedding dress and billowing tulle veil, which hung in solitary splendour. Everything else was packed or had been moved to Mike's flat. The room had already taken on an unoccupied appearance.

Molly had moved out too, and no doubt was now waking up at home in Brooklyn, thinking about her big day. Annie smiled. Funny to think that she and Molly were getting married in a double ceremony. What fun they had had planning what they would wear. Molly's mother had come up trumps with a clever dressmaker who had worked no small miracle in her ability to copy the very fashionable wedding gowns currently on show in New York's most exclusive stores. While Annie had opted for a white satin dress fashioned in simple lines, Molly had chosen white organdy with ruffles on the neck and sleeves. Both would wear tulle veils.

No doubt if she and Mike had not been planning to travel out to Arizona straight after Christmas, they would have waited a few months to marry. But it would not have been seemly to make the long journey alone together if they were unmarried, so it seemed perfectly proper – Tom being Annie's brother – to make it a double occasion with him and Molly. It was also more fun, and four heads seemed a lot better than two when it came to organising it all. It was all the more perfect that Mike and Tom were as close to one another as she and Molly were.

Annie thought back to the day she had first met Mike. It was on the tender sailing out from Queenstown to board the steamship for America, exactly seven years ago. She recalled how, just as they drew level with the huge ship outside the harbour, a handsome young man with a friendly smile had appeared out of nowhere, effortlessly lifted her trunk and carried it on board for her. She had taken to him instantly.

He had already emigrated to America, he had told her, but had come back to Ireland briefly for his brother's ordination and was returning to New York, where he worked as a tailor. Then he wished her good luck and was gone.

As he was travelling in the men's quarters, she never caught even a glimpse of him again during the voyage, but he appeared at her side again on the morning they arrived in New York and he helped her alight from the ship. Somehow, with all the excitement of being the first passenger to land at the new Ellis Island station and being awarded the special ten-dollar gold piece followed by the joy of being reunited with her parents, she had lost sight of him.

She had thought about him many times during those first lonely months in New York, wondering what sort of life he led in the bustling metropolis. Then, as suddenly as he had first come into her life, he re-entered it. As she had been going to collect her young brother Philip from night school one evening, a chivalrous young man had held the door of the school open for her to pass. It was none other than Mike Tierney, who taught upholstery there on two evenings a week.

'Well, if it isn't the famous golden-dollar girl,' he had teased. From that moment they had become friends. Although only fifteen at the time, Annie had instantly fallen in love with him. But to Mike she was like a younger sister. How she had despaired in those days that he would ever come to love her. Strange that she had never become discouraged – well, perhaps she had once or twice – and continued, even when she lived out in Nebraska, to hope that one day he would return her love. No other young man had ever seriously captured her heart, though they had tried. Carl had come closest and there was a time when, full sure that she had lost Mike to someone else, she had almost promised herself to Carl. But then, very suddenly – as was his wont – Mike had appeared in Nebraska, intent on winning her, and everything had come right at last.

A feeling of sadness came over Annie momentarily, thinking of Carl, killed so tragically in the war. And then her thoughts turned to Sophia. Strange how she would always link these two in death, and yet they had never even met.

How different her life would be from now on. She would not miss New York now so much, with her only remaining link with the Lower East Side, Sophia, gone. She was ready for change. She longed to start her life as Mike's partner. Here they were, on the threshold of a great joint adventure –

leaving the city and setting off together into the deserts of Arizona to start a new life. She wondered would they be blessed with children. Would they ever return to Ireland? She and Mike had discussed these things and yes, he wanted children, he said, lots of them – all little golden-haired angels like his golden girl.

As for returning to Ireland, they hoped they would do so one day. Their children must see the land of their forefathers, Mike said. Cork and Tipperary. What a faraway sound they had now. Julia Donohue had written a letter of good wishes and continuing affection but somehow it had the same faraway feel. Would she even know Julia now if she saw her?

'Annie,' Aunt Norah broke in on her reveries and stood smiling sleepily at her niece. 'You'd better get up, love. You don't want to be late for that man of yours, now do you?'

Dear Auntie Norah! How well she and Charlie looked. Gone was that frail look she'd always had, and Charlie was as brown as a nut. Both of them were full of enthusiasm about their new life. They'd all sat up until the small hours on the night of their arrival, hearing all the family news and heeding advice about what to bring and what they shouldn't bother with.

How thankful she was that her family would be part of this new adventure, that they had all somehow managed to stay together. As a little girl, parted early (though temporarily) from her parents, that had been her greatest worry. How fortunate, too, that they had taken Mike to their hearts as one of their own. Mike had no family in America and she knew he missed them sorely from time to time. How glad she was for him that his brother Sean would be with them for the wedding. And the fact that he would marry them made his visit all the more special.

Hearing Uncle Charlie hum 'The Sidewalks of New York' in the bathroom, Annie knew it was time to meet the new day.

Looking out of the window, she was delighted to see snow falling softly. 'A real white wedding it'll be,' she laughed.

'Well, make the most of it, *a stór*, you won't see much of that where you're going,' said Auntie Norah, as she served breakfast to her niece in the tiny kitchen.

Father Sean's deep, sonorous voice, with its familiar Irish lilt, seemed to echo around the small church as he uttered the most solemn words of the marriage rite.

Annie repeated them, her voice clear for all to hear. 'I, Annie Moore, take you, Mike Tierney, for my husband, to have and to hold, from this day forward, for better, for worse, for richer, for poorer, in sickness and in health, until death do us part.'

Vows exchanged, Mike took the simple gold ring from his best man and placed it on her outstretched finger.

'With this ring, I thee wed,' he said, looking down at her, his eyes alight with love.

Then it was Tom and Molly's turn to

exchange vows, and it wasn't long until both couples found themselves in the sacristy signing the register and being congratulated heartily by Father Sean and the wedding party. Then the organ struck up Wagner's triumphant wedding march and they proceeded down the aisle of the church, emerging into the dazzling winter sunshine, to be greeted with joy by relatives and friends alike.

The wedding breakfast at the Excelsior Hotel was a resounding success. The manager – Tom's boss – made sure everything ran smoothly and that they were all treated like royalty.

The speeches and the toasts over, Anthony stood up to read out the telegrams, which, with two couples to be felicitated, were numerous. But the one which meant the most to Annie and to her brother Tom was the one from their parents and Philip in Arizona.

Wish we could be with you all today STOP Our

thoughts and prayers with you as you take this big step STOP Health and happiness to you always STOP Love Father, Mother Philip STOP

That over, Uncle Charlie announced that the entertainment was about to begin. Irrepressible as ever, he had brought his banjo from Arizona, and along with one of Tom's friends who had brought his fiddle, they struck up some lively music.

Her hand in Mike's, Annie sat contentedly watching everyone enjoy themselves. How good it was to see Ellie and Dan looking as happy as ever, chatting animatedly to Uncle Charlie. And Alice Rodgers and Mike's charming best man, Billy Farrelly, seemed to be hitting it off very well indeed. And there was Auntie Norah and Molly's mother Hannah with their heads together, looking as if they had been friends all their lives.

To Annie's great joy, Sophia's parents had come to the wedding. She had worried that they would find it a trial to see their daughter's friend marry the man she loved while their beloved Sophia was lost to them forever. But she need not have fretted, because if they were suffering, they concealed it very well. Mr Rostov was deep in conversation with Mike's brother, Father Sean, and his wife seemed to be enjoying Tom and Molly's company.

Anthony was outdoing himself, trying to impress Ellie's niece Laura, who was looking very pretty in a chic little hat – of her own creation, naturally. To Annie's delight, Auntie Norah had promised to introduce Laura to her old boss, the head of the Millinery Department in A. & T. Stewart's, before she returned to Arizona.

'Order, order!' called Uncle Charlie, who took his role as host very seriously indeed. 'It's time now for the dancing to begin. So if the two bridegrooms would lead out their lovely brides...'

Mike led Annie slowly out onto the dance floor and Tom followed with Molly. New York's two happiest young couples led the dancing, their feet scarcely touching the ground. Swinging her around expertly, Mike's eyes glowed as he looked down at his Annie.

'My wife,' he whispered into her gold curls, which now swung loose and free. 'My golden girl.'

Annie and Mike leant out of the carriage window as the night express pulled slowly out of Grand Central Station, waving to those who had come to see them off and who were now receding further and further into the distance. For all her newfound happiness, Annie's eyes were blurred with tears. Dearest Molly and Tom, and Anthony. When would she see them again?

Sensing her sadness, Mike drew her gently away from the window and pulled down the sash.

Having removed her new hat and placed it carefully on the overhead rack above their luggage, Annie sat down and smoothed out her new travelling costume. Looking across at her smiling husband, she reached for his hand and placed a small box in his open palm.

'All my worldly goods,' she said softly.

His expression changing to one of surprise and wonder, Mike opened it to discover a shining ten-dollar gold piece.

'Seven years ago today, you cleared the way for me to step onto American soil,' his wife explained. 'I've kept it ever since to share with you. I know it will bring us luck.'

EPILOGUE

Readers of my three fictional books about Annie Moore might be interested to know what happened to the real Annie Moore after her arrival in America on 1 January 1892. As is well known, Annie was the first immigrant of any nationality to set foot on American soil at Ellis Island on the day the new Immigration Centre opened there. Because of this, she received a special commemorative ten-dollar gold piece from the welcoming party of dignitaries who had assembled to mark the occasion. It was also her fifteenth birthday – an auspicious beginning for a young Irish emigrant.

There is not a great deal of information about what happened to Annie after her arrival, but some facts have been established. After some time in New York, the family moved west to Indiana, where Annie met Patrick O'Connell, said to be a descendant of Irish liberator Daniel O'Connell. She married Pat O'Connell in Texas in 1898 when she was twenty-one years old. The Moore family had moved to Waco in central Texas to farm.

After her marriage, it was discovered that Annie's lungs were weak and she and her husband moved to Fort Worth in west Texas. The O'Connells then moved further west again, to Clovis, New Mexico, where they owned a hotel and restaurant beside the then-thriving railroad. Unfortunately, Annie lost her husband in the great influenza epidemic in 1919.

She and her older children managed the property after Pat's death and it grew into a successful enterprise. Then tragedy struck again. In 1923, Annie was travelling to Fort Worth in Texas to visit her younger brother Pat, and was knocked down and killed by one of the first rapid-transit trains.

Her children were quite young – the

youngest only five years old – when they were orphaned. They were taken in and reared by their aunts and uncles in Fort Worth, Texas.

Eithne Loughrey

This Large Print Book, for people
who cannot read normal print,
is published under the auspices of
THE ULVERSCROFT FOUNDATION